Praise for *Mothers Don't*

"A wholly incomplete but no less emphatic list of the ways that Katixa Agirre's *Mothers Don't* is extraordinary: it never stops moving; the writing is sharp, intoxicating; the pacing balletic; it weaves together the personal and intimate with the procedural, psychiatric, and philosophical; it asks consternating questions and posits fascinating contradictions, but never pretends that any of life—and least of all motherhood and art—might deign to make any kind of sense."

—Lynn Steger Strong

"It might seem that everything has already been said about the experience of motherhood and its darkest reverse sides, but *Mothers Don't* shows that there are still many corners to explore, and it does it with accuracy and intelligence."

—Aixa de la Cruz

"Fascinating. Addictive. Agirre dares to name things that I have thought, but would never dare to say."

—̄mma Suárez

"Takes your breatl  ous."

Hernández

"*Mothers Don't* is first-rate literature: psychological but carefree."

—Juan Marqués, *El Mundo*

MOTHERS DON'T

Katixa Agirre

Translated from the Spanish by Katie Whittemore

Curated by Katie Whittemore for the 2022 Translator Triptych

OPEN LETTER
LITERARY TRANSLATIONS FROM THE UNIVERSITY OF ROCHESTER

Originally published in Basque as *Amek ez dute* by Elkar, and in Spanish as *Las madres no* by Tránsito

Copyright © 2018, 2019 by Katixa Agirre

Translation copyright © 2022 by Katie Whittemore

Published in arrangement with The Ella Sher Literary Agency

www.ellasher.com

Library of Congress Cataloging-in-Publication Data: Available.

ISBN-13: 9781948830560

Ebook ISBN: 9781948830621

This project is supported in part by an award from the National Endowment for the Arts and the New York State Council on the Arts with the support of the Governor of New York State and the New York State Legislature.

Support for the translation of this book was provided by Acción Cultural Española, AC/E

Printed on acid-free paper in the United States of America

Cover Design by Anne Jordan

Interior Design by Anuj Mathur

Open Letter is the University of Rochester's nonprofit, literary translation press:

Dewey Hall 1-219, Box 278968, Rochester NY 14627

www.openletterbooks.org

Contents

PART I

CREATION

1.

THE REVELATION

Go inside children; all will be fine.

EURIPIDES, *Medea*

It happened at the height of summer.

A Thursday afternoon.

That day, the nanny walked through the front gate to the house in Armentia like a person opening the gates of Hell: reluctantly, cheeks flushed. As usual, her four free hours on Thursday afternoon had flown by. The girl's name was Mèlanie and she had been in Vitoria for nine months, learning Spanish and evaluating her "next step" in life. She locked her bike up around the back, tried to wipe the mud off her sandals, and apprehensively entered the house. It was quiet; she cast a wary glance into the kitchen, then the living room, then the room that occasionally functioned as a studio for the lady of the house. Nothing. That was a good sign. She allowed her thoughts to wander back to the boy she'd spent the afternoon with, the one who had invited her on a bike ride through Salburua park. He was all right, but ...

She didn't signal her presence or call out to her employer. Instead she moved stealthily, in case the twins were sleeping—a remote possibility, after all she knew perfectly well they were light

3

sleepers. But if by some miracle the twins *were* peacefully asleep, she might have time to take a shower, a nice, long, warm, shower. Her shorts and ankles were caked in mud. When she'd lain down with the boy in the park, she hadn't noticed the grass was wet.

She removed her sandals before going up the carpeted stairs. It was there, on the last step, where she felt the vibration. It was a feeling she would have immediately forgotten, if it hadn't been for what happened next. Later, she would describe it as the flight instinct: she had a vision of herself on her bicycle, racing downhill at full speed and never, ever looking back. It wasn't the first occasion such an urge had struck her since she'd worked in the house, but she didn't succumb to it this time either. Why should she? Instead, she continued down the hallway to her employers' bedroom. The door was ajar. She held her breath. Furtively, she peered inside and spotted two little bundles on the parents' bed. The duvet covered them almost completely. She could hardly make out the two little heads. The twins. Their eyes were closed. Beside the bed, in an armchair upholstered in striped fabric, sat Alice Espanet, the mother, dressed in a nightgown. One of her breasts was exposed. The left.

The nanny, a twenty-two-year-old au pair from Orleans, France—who up until then had been a happy, rather silly girl—said nothing, or didn't remember later if she had. She did, however, approach the bed, her mind completely blank as she took the five tremulous steps, each more ominous than the last. She did not look at the mother, she couldn't. She felt empty, erased, evaporated, completely absent for the first time in her short life.

She just barely touched the bundles. Half a second was long enough. The twins weren't moving, and they weren't asleep. Purple lips, cold skin. They were naked. The sheet, still damp.

"They're fine now." Mèlanie jumped at the sound of the mother's voice, though she spoke with perfect calm. The voice struck her as terrible, unbearable.

Even worse was her manner: placid, almost listless, indolent.

From the nightstand the nanny picked up the phone, the same phone she used to call France on the very rare occasion she found herself alone. But this time, she placed a distressed call for an ambulance, an army of police officers, firemen, anybody, as fast as they could, please, please hurry. The conversation was recorded and that's how we know it lasted two minutes, that there were some challenges with communication, sighs, wailing, disbelief. To all appearances, Alice Espanet kept her composure for the duration of the call. She didn't move from the armchair, or cover her left breast.

When the dispatcher on the other end of the line finally understood the magnitude of what had happened, the machinery was set into motion: before long—still an eternity—the house in Armentia was crawling with people. The house itself was large but unpretentious. Alice and her husband had moved in when it was brand new, just four years earlier and after much vexation on account of a certain famous architect's lack of reliability. When the chaos descended, Mèlanie waited outside on the front steps, hugging her knees, studying the mud on her ankles. They made her come into the kitchen and take a seat. They asked her questions. She tried to answer; she could barely breathe, much less speak. Someone brought her a glass of water. Another friendly hand passed her a small white pill. She swallowed without asking what it was.

For hours, lights from the ambulance and patrol cars flashed across the home's façade. From a distance, it must have looked like some kind of party or grand opening, and more than a few neighbors, runners, and passersby stopped to investigate. It was a warm summer evening, not at all common in Vitoria, perfectly suited for an al fresco *akelarre*. No one except Mèlanie wanted to leave, especially as the rumors spread and grew even more atrocious.

The father—Ricardo to his clients and Ritxi to his friends—arrived just ten minutes before the investigating judge, a day's worth of sweat still on his skin. At the exact moment Mèlanie was entering the house, thinking about the end of her afternoon off, Ritxi was leaving Madrid in a chauffeured car. He arrived in time to witness the twins' little bodies being placed into giant, gray bags. He was also witness to how they put his wife in the back of a patrol car, hastily dressed in leggings and a loose T-shirt she wore when doing yoga. They hadn't cuffed her. This was somehow comforting to Ritxi. He shouted her name, just the once, but she didn't look over. Inside the car, she kept her head high, her neck stiff. A Eurydice made of salt.

They gave Ritxi the name of a hospital. Seventh floor. Psychiatric evaluation. Later, he too was offered a little white pill, but he swatted it away, sending it flying under the couch where it would remain, maybe forever.

No one saw him cry.

The nanny came over to tell him she would be staying with a friend for the night.

Ritxi waved her off, so Mèlanie got ready to flee on her bike at last, which is what she should have done all along. Unfortunately, she didn't get the chance this time either: she would need to go with the police, there were a lot of questions to get through. They kept her at the station until her tears ran out and the police were satisfied. Only then could she escape. Shortly thereafter, she left the country. She moved to Paris, where for a time she tried to find acting work. When she learned fourteen months later that she would have to testify at the trial, she had a panic attack.

Ritxi's parents were dead. His only brother lived in the U.S. He rejected all offers of help from on-call psychologists and well-meaning friends. He wanted to stay in the house, he wanted to be alone. He was so emphatic that they had to let him. It was well past midnight. His statement could wait till morning.

In the meantime, he disconnected the phones.

The next morning at eight on the dot, two officers of the

ertzaintza reported to the house in Armentia, and a composed Ritxi—"too composed, to be honest," one of the officers would later declare—opened the oak front door. They were very sorry to disturb him, but his statement was crucial, he would have to accompany them and answer a few questions. Ritxi asked for two minutes to change his shirt—he was still wearing the button-down from yesterday's business trip to Madrid, sweat and all—and invited the officers inside.

When he finished, they were ready to go.

By the time the news reached editorial offices, it was too late to make the nightly broadcasts. Its impact the next day, however, was thunderous: it was the middle of the summer and the media worried the story like a dog with a bone. It became the only item on the agenda. The truth is that now, in the second decade of the twenty-first century, murder is an anomaly. Murder is—at most—something men perpetrate against their partners or exes. A kind of ineluctable baseline. This is why some murders in particular inspire so much curiosity, so many clicks, such high ratings; especially the ones *not* committed by men against women.

The furor reached my ears, of course. At first, I tried to avoid the news. Change the channel, turn the page, close the window. If someone mentioned the case in my presence, I tried to switch topics: it was so hot, so unusually hot, and I clung to the weather as an excuse to shift the conversation.

Most people understood it wasn't an appropriate topic to discuss when I was in earshot. But there were always the less considerate: at the butcher, the hairdresser, a wedding. All sorts of places, really.

The subject was just so lurid—even more so given my condition. I didn't know how to react to the news, so I ignored it. It was an active, conscious effort; a challenge I met with decent success.

Then two weeks later, that radically changed.

Just two weeks after Alice Espanet (allegedly) killed her twin babies, the incident was becoming a gray, gooey memory in the minds of pundits and upstanding citizens. The flowers laid by the compassionate in front of the house in Armentia were wilting, the stuffed animals left for the children losing their luster. As for me, I was completely removed from the whole thing, trapped in Basurto Hospital's brand-new Obstetrics Unit. The prostaglandin tampon was beginning to take effect and I was experiencing my first contractions. I was in the early stages of induced labor, hooked up to a monitor, sure that what awaited me was, frankly, unimaginable pain or—in the words of Hélène Deutsch—"an orgy of masochistic pleasure." (I had dedicated the previous months to reading everything about giving birth I could get my hands on, even that caliber of nonsense.)

As anticipated, I myself experienced no pleasure, no masochism, and certainly no orgy of any kind.

Yet I did experience, in the most unexpected of ways, a revelation. A revelation that would determine, if not the rest of my life (out of deference for the child about to be born), then at least the next two or three years of it.

The function of contractions in labor is not entirely understood. Some claim the agony is a biblical curse, while others say we're conditioned to feel the pain by a misogynistic society. Considering the dearth of scientific evidence, one could say that the physiology of labor is still a big unknown in medicine, as is often the case when women's bodies are involved. There has been some suggestion that this specific kind of pain is the only way the body manages to directly access the paleocortex, the primitive brain. Over time, humans have added layers and layers of reasoning to this primitive brain, ultimately creating the neocortex: our modern brain. And if you allow the neocortex to get involved in childbirth, the process becomes mission impossible. No, what you have to do is reclaim the reptilian instinct, return to the jungle, banish verbal language, the ability to walk upright on two legs. Labor is made tenable only by forgetting evolution, traveling millions of years back in time. This, then, is the purpose of the pain: knock out the neocortex, deactivate it, so we can feel like powerful female gorillas in the jungles of Africa.

It's just a hunch, but maybe it explains why I reacted the way I did when offered an epidural by the first midwife. That bitch wanted to use her anesthesia to pull me out of the jungle. Actually, she was a very sweet woman. She called me *honey*.

"You've been doing great, honey. You're fully effaced and three centimeters dilated. We can bring you for the epidural whenever you're ready."

"No! Fuck no!"

Like I said, in that instant, I was a female gorilla in the jungle. You don't talk to gorillas. Language takes us to the neocortex.

I imagine she wasn't offended by my outburst, good professional that she was, and I sincerely do regret saying it. I blame the paleocortex for my foul mouth. And what came next, too. Three more contractions and then came the mother of them all, an irrepressible wave that swept me straight into another dimension, another place, another era (torches instead of lamps, togas instead of doctors' white coats) and bam, I had THE REVELATION.

Eleven years ago, I met Alice Espanet, the (allegedly) insane, merciless killer. That's right! Of course! Not only had I met her, but we'd lived across the hall from each other for a few weeks. The thing was, back then she hadn't gone by Alice. It came to me all at once, plunged in that whirlwind of pain. Given how hard I'd tried to avoid the images in the press and how she hadn't crossed my mind since the last time I saw her, I hadn't recognized her at first. That, and the fact that eleven years do leave their mark on a person. But the combination of prostaglandin and oxytocin—combined with the activated paleocortex's atavistic knowing—had revealed a truth: I'd associated with that (allegedly) abominable woman when I was young and green and still knew almost nothing of pain.

The revelation took my breath away.

But it turns out that in order to bear the contractions with any kind of dignity, one needs to be in control of her breath. They teach that in all childbirth preparation courses. Breathe in one, two, breathe out one, two, three, four. It's a mantra. Lose the rhythm and then it's curtains for you. Pain takes hold, thrashes you against a thorny bush. Has its way with you. You lose confidence in yourself. You're no gorilla now: you are a pathetic rag doll. A scrap.

I did ask for the epidural in the end, once THE REVELA-TION broke my focus. The midwife who called me honey had already finished her shift, which I was glad about.

As the anesthesia spread throughout my body, I told myself that I had to hang on to THE REVELATION at all costs. I'm not really sure why I attributed amnesiac effects to the anesthesia. It doesn't have them, and I managed to remember everything.

Seven hours later, Erik was born. He was very small, a tiny thing weighing just over two kilos, hot and messy. They laid him on my chest and his body stamped a Lanzarote-shaped stain on my sternum. Then, moments of confusion, clamor, disbelief: the baby was taken from me immediately. The delivery room was suddenly packed with people (had it been all along?) and everyone seemed to be in a rush. As I stroked the empty space on my breastbone left by my human pup, I was bombarded with words I was unversed in at the time, words like *Apgar test, meconium stain*. What they were really saying was *you aren't getting the baby back for a while*. During the final weeks of pregnancy, the fetus had been diagnosed with the initials SGA, but the gynecologist who ordered my induction had changed the diagnosis to IUGR. Although these letters don't mean anything to me now, suffice it to say that IUGR is worse than SGA, hence the urgency to get the baby out of my womb. Whereas SGA means that the baby is small, IUGR elbows in and proclaims that the baby is *too* small. In any case, according to what the gynecologist assured me before leaving me in the hands of a very attractive hospital porter, everything would be fine: at Week 38, the pregnancy could be considered done and dusted without further complications.

"Don't worry, in most cases, the babies don't even need the incubator," the doctor said, sealing my fate and dispatching me to Obstetrics.

And basically, so it was. The baby didn't need to be incubated. Eight hours in the neonatal unit and away from me were enough. Coming in at two palpitating kilos, he was the biggest baby in the room, according to reports from Niclas, who was able to visit him a few times and take pictures. I wasn't allowed to go anywhere, not with half my body still numb.

Niclas returned from the NICU emotional, his joy tinged with angst—hence the obsessive repetition of *it's unbelievable, but he's the biggest one in there*—zooming in on the pictures, absorbing every detail, until I told him I was tired, to give me a little peace. I was exhausted, but I couldn't manage to sleep. I lay on my side in the hospital bed and all I could think about was Alice Espanet. Jade Espanet, when I knew her. Maybe it was a trick of the psyche, a way to not dwell on Erik, feign that I wasn't worried and that everything would be fine. Every once in a while I checked to make sure the Lanzarote-shaped stain was still there. I brought my nose to my chest and tried to capture that sweet, novel scent.

Erik was finally brought to me at nightfall. He had been bathed, but still had that penetrating, suddenly familiar smell. He was like a little bun, fresh out of the oven, and I wanted to eat him up. Literally.

A pediatrician went over the testing and bloodwork endured by his tiny body. Erik had Band-Aids on his thighs where the needles had punctured his skin, but apparently he'd been given sugar water as an analgesic. The truth was that I didn't want to know anything about what had happened during the hours we were apart; I just wanted to hear that everything was fine. And it was. Basically, he was small. For reasons unknown—*There's still a lot we don't know about pregnancy*, the pediatrician said humbly—at some point he'd stopped gaining weight, maybe even lost a gram or two there at the end, and that's why he was better off out of the womb. Now he would eat and grow and "catch up" and whatever else about percentages and unintelligible abbreviations.

Hoping I could follow the lactation consultant's confusing instructions, I brought the baby to my breast. And this was, more or less, my principle undertaking for the following months. I was an amorphous thing attached to two big tits, where a tiny, beautiful boy was attached in turn.

At least, that was the image I presented on the outside. If somebody had pried into my interior, they would have found the creases and crevices were more plentiful, and quite a bit darker. I had stitches between my legs—just a first-degree tear, but still—and my nipples were raw. I was suffering from my first case of hemorrhoids, my arms and legs were still sore from the final stage of labor, and, thanks to an as yet undiagnosed case of anemia, I felt flimsier than an autumn leaf.

I was aching and wrecked, and there was nothing for me to capitalize on inside that pain, that physical devastation. And yet, just beyond pain's borders, Jade/Alice circled day and night. And I knew I had no choice: I had to immerse myself in the inquietude. I am a writer, after all, and that's our only clear mandate. Besides, given my state at the time, it was easy to surrender to my obsession. I was at its mercy and that seemed just fine to me.

And so, once we were back at home with the baby and I had a free hand (while the baby nursed, of course) one of the first things I did was text Léa, a college friend. Although we had only lived in the same student residence for a year, some eleven years ago, and despite the fact that she lived in France, we'd managed to keep in good touch. By email at first, then Facebook, and during the final weeks of my pregnancy, at my friend's insistence, we had moved to Telegram. It was via this third platform that I sent her a picture of my newborn (without including—as many mothers do for reasons that escape me—his measurements).

Erik's here, all is well.

Léa wrote right back with congratulations and every color of heart emoji.

For a few minutes, my phone vibrated with a flurry of conversation. She asked me how I was doing, if labor had been hard. I said it hadn't, really, without going into details that would distract me from my true mission. The device went still. It took me a few minutes to summon my courage, then a couple more to find the right words.

I heard about Jade.

Silence.

Had some chore distracted her from reading the message? Was she struck dumb by the horror of what had occurred? Or maybe she didn't know—after all, it had happened across the border, she might have already lost contact with Jade, Jade wasn't called Jade anymore, etc.—and was simply waiting for me to clue her in on what the Hell I was talking about.

Silence.

It was the first time I brought up the case with another person. In hopes it would incubate properly, I'd chosen not to air it with anyone. Not even Niclas. But now Léa, whom I had chosen (and needed) as a confidante, was cruelly failing me. It couldn't be. Unable to bear the anxiety, I switched Erik to the other breast before I'd made sure he was done.

Still no reply from Léa.

I kept waiting. I had no other purpose, no other horizon in life. The baby sucked and sucked on my searing nipples, which I now bore with resignation.

The phone dinged.

How did you hear?

So she knew. The news had reached Avignon. Of course it had. A French woman drowns her infant twins in Spain. An incomprehensible murder. Profiles of Jade/Alice. Morbid details, real or invented. The recollections of childhood neighbors. The media had gotten a hold of the story there, too. I quickly explained that it had happened close to where I lived, not more than sixty-five kilometers away (I recalled that geography wasn't Léa's strong suit: when I first mentioned Bilbao to her, she had been convinced it was a city in Portugal), and that the news had caused a huge stir.

We're in shock. I don't know what to say.

She didn't add anything else.

Erik reared back his little head, the signal that he was all done feeding. Fingers trembling, I reclasped my nursing bra and laid him on my shoulder to begin what we colloquially referred to as *flatulence on parade.*

Léa, generally speaking, was an incessant talker. She'd been like that when I met her at the university in England, and that was how she'd been throughout our ensuing long-distance friendship. And now, right now, she had chosen to leave me in suspense: either she didn't understand my thirst, or was refusing to quench it. What was going on? Did I need to push a little harder?

Obviously, I did.

I can imagine. We'll talk another time then. XO.

I bid her a graceful adieu, but left the door wide open to resume the conversation (another time = as soon as possible), and wound down the flatulence parade more quickly than usual. Erik, attuned to my agitation, rid himself of gas in record time then fell right to sleep: a fantastic nap lasting all of twelve minutes.

We met in the heart of England, in the region called the Midlands. The university was new, small, born of the Further and Higher Education Act passed in the early 90s. It specialized in sports, business, and communication. Faculty members' offices were located in two single-story pavilions that had served as a hospital during World War II. The howls of amputees could still be heard in those halls, all those years later. Our entire existence revolved around the campus: we lived in one of the student residences, and got drunk at the dance club where the next day we worked for four and a half quid an hour cleaning. We were happy in an uncomplicated way.

I arrived on September 8th. Léa arrived the next day. We lived across the hall from each other, I was in Apartment A and Léa in B. We usually propped open our doors with fire extinguishers, which made it feel like we were living in one big Apartment AB. There was always activity in our hallway. We also tended to leave the doors to our respective bedrooms open, as you never knew when the opportunity to do something might come up. It was impossible to find time to be alone, but I don't remember missing it. Laughter, tears, promiscuity with zero discretion. That's how I remember that brief but beautiful time, an intense but nonetheless pleasant version of life.

Léa didn't come on her own. A friend joined her, to help her settle in those first days. Léa had brought a lot of luggage, and apparently a porter was indispensable. The porter was named Jade. I didn't pay much attention to the pair of French girls at first, to be honest. And I paid even less attention when I learned that one of them was essentially a tag-along. I was new to the campus, to the city, to the country. I was looking for friendships that could last the whole year; I couldn't waste my time on people just passing through. When you're living overseas, especially if you have to survive in a language you haven't yet mastered, you have to make optimal use of your resources. It's also true that while

Jade's beauty was striking—her cat eyes—she didn't prove to be especially friendly and her English was almost indecipherable. *Ai!* when she wanted to say *Hi!*, for example.

I have two specific memories of her: standing on the landing between Apartments A and B, hidden behind Léa, and at one of the first parties—held in C, if memory serves—a naïve smile on her face, plastic cup in hand, surrounded by half a dozen guys of assorted origins. Apart from that, nothing.

I'd been digging through my recollections since the day of THE REVELATION and by that point my memory was an empty mine. *Ai!* and her feline eyes. It would have to satisfy me, for the time being. She was just a girl who had passed through my life, hardly leaving a mark. Pity. But what was I hoping for? A malevolent gleam in twenty-one-year-old Jade's eye to rise to the surface of my brain so I could promptly trace all possible twists the story offered, reveal some kind of causal logic—our meeting, her deviance, the dead children? Obviously not, right? So why did I feel so disappointed?

The day of my fruitless conversation with Léa, I had a strange dream during Erik's twenty-minute evening nap. In the dream, Erik was hanging from my breast, the right one. A hungry Jade was trying to drink from the other. To stop her from suckling, I smacked her forehead with a wooden spoon while repeating *Fiche-moi la paix, putain!* in a perfect Parisian accent, despite the fact that I don't speak French.

I usually tend not to put much stock in my dreams, but I must confess, that sudden case of xenoglossia disturbed me for quite some time.

2.

THE DECISION

Mothers do not write, they are written.

SUSAN SULEIMAN

In the fall of that same year, when motherhood had physically and psychologically sucked me dry, when I'd managed to get Erik into the third percentile (which earned him the distinction of "normal") and left irreversible wear and tear on my nipples as a consequence, I received a truly enormous surprise.

While taking our habitual twenty-minute morning nap, Erik and I were interrupted by a phone call. I answered a tad aggressively, assuming it was some telemarketer from the other side of the world (in that period, nobody contacted me of his or her own volition, they imagined I was busy, tied up, didn't want to be bothered, etc.). Instead, a somewhat cowed voice claimed to be calling from the Basque Government's Department of Culture. Apparently, they wanted to give me a prize. The Euskadi Prize. Would I accept it? I looked down at the screen, then returned the phone to my ear and said:

"Yeah right!"

Fortunately, the voice on the other end of the line ignored my

17

reaction and went on to explain the next steps by rote: if I accepted the prize, I would have to appear at a press conference and attend the award ceremony several weeks later, where I'd have to say a few words. I would be photographed. The Basque President and Minister of Culture would be there. A small banquet to follow. Then home.

Both the press conference and the award ceremony would be held in Vitoria.

"Okay, but for which book?"

The bureaucrat on duty didn't deign to respond. Which was fortunate, because it was an idiotic question: I had only written one book, a political thriller published a year and a half before. Just then, Erik started to cry, saving me from the situation. I rushed off the phone, promising to call back as soon as I could. I walked around with the baby and composed myself. Was this really happening? With Erik in my arms, I googled the phone number that had called. It turned out that yes, it was indeed a Basque government number. I took a breath. I thought about jumping up and down, but judged that jumping (even a little) would be detrimental to my pelvic floor.

The book, my now award-winning book, followed the final steps (perhaps "final strides" would be more exact) of the Basque separatist group ETA's only victim from the United States; and, in parallel, focused on the lives of the three members of the cell that ended his life.

My novel began in a middle-class suburb in New Jersey. Eugene Kenneth Brown (Gene, to family and friends) bid a tender goodbye to his wife and children. An inventory control specialist for Johnson & Johnson, Brown set off for Newark Airport with a small suitcase. That same day, somebody stole a Peugeot 505 in the Donostian neighborhood of Amara. That Peugeot, with a fake license plate, headed toward Madrid. Gene landed at Barajas Airport. The Peugeot reached its destination. In a Madrid apartment, we are introduced to two men and one woman. In addition to their daily routines, they built a bomb, placed in it the Peugeot, and parked the car on Calle Carbonero y Sol.

The woman and the men appeared under their real names in the novel, since the three had become well-known to the public in the years following the murder. One of the men, remorseful, would describe the details of this attack and others. The second because, once he'd completed his sentence, a Socialist minister proclaimed that he would "build a new indictment" against him; and in effect, that's what happened, the result being the prisoner on hunger strike and violence in the streets. As for the woman, she became famous as a negotiator with the Spanish government in the Algiers and Switzerland negotiations, in 1989 and 1999, respectively. Violence erupts in the third part of the book, breaking completely from the slow pace of the preceding pages. As a Guardia Civil convoy passes by, there's an explosion, which doesn't entirely reach the agents of the Benemérita. To complete the mission, the terrorists fired at the wounded officers. Their aim was awful. That's when the reinforcements arrived, other *guardias* working security at the nearby Soviet embassy. They started shooting as well. It's a long episode, hyperreal, inspired by war reporting.

Finally, the shooting ends, the smoke clears, and a body is visible, the only body found in the midst of all that chaos: Eugene Kenneth Brown, inventory control specialist for Johnson & Johnson, in Madrid on business, still wearing his running shoes. He had gone out to give his legs a bit of a stretch before boarding the plane back to Newark.

All sorts of things were said about my novel *Inventario*: that it whitewashed ETA's crimes by presenting the *etarras* as people (human beings who ate strawberries, took showers, and repressed their sexuality); that it indiscriminately repeated the war propaganda of the Madrid cell; that it took a kinder view of the female character simply because she was a woman; that it dragged the good name of a hero for peace through the mud; that it exploited morbid curiosity; that it didn't take the ETA's other victims into account; that it didn't talk about torture by the Guardia Civil; that I was nothing but a bloodsucking parasite feeding off the Basque conflict while it was still in vogue.

The humble controversy, in any case, was good for the book, which was in its seventh printing after a year and a half. The commercial success further irritated professional critics and amateurs alike—really nasty things were said about me on Twitter, which affected me in the beginning—and their reactions continued to boost sales in a vicious cycle that was quite pleasant to watch. Soon the Spanish translation arrived thanks to a small, kind of hipster yet prestigious press in Barcelona. Attention heated up when a leftist representative from Madrid made a laudatory comment about the novel, and lawmakers from the other side accused him of reading literature that colluded with terrorism. The book enjoyed a not-insignificant spike in sales that week. Shortly thereafter, versions in Catalan and Hungarian came out, with a Polish translator "working around the clock." My agent assured me that a deal for an English translation was about to happen, and around the same time, I signed over the film rights, which didn't bring in a single euro for me but generated plenty of naïve excitement. I was very busy. I was asked to give talks in the Basque County's most elegant auditoriums. I was also offered a platform to speak in the most charming bookstores in Madrid, Barcelona, and Menorca. I went to Liverpool to teach a seminar on literature and the Basque conflict. I had to turn down a chance to participate in the Frankfurt Book Fair because I calculated that Erik would be too small for us to be apart. I won awards. I was profiled in newspapers, magazines, online. Every time a notable Basque cultural figure died, some journalist would call me and ask for my opinion.

Remembering that whole tempest was like looking back on a remote epoch (torches, togas . . .).

So, I didn't jump with joy at the news. Instead, I remained stunned for a half hour. I picked up the baby, returned him to his crib. He was finally asleep, but I didn't dare call the Cultural Office back. What was behind my unease? The book was already long behind me, to such an extent that it no longer even felt like my own. Not only that: remembering that at one point it *had* been the center of my life was mortifying. And now—now!—they were going to give me a prize for it, and not just any prize, but the highest honor in Basque letters. It was absolutely absurd.

When the book had first appeared in bookstores, I would stand near the display windows and observe peoples' faces in hopes of ascertaining whether those strangers knew that I was the author of *Inventario*. It should have been obvious, right? Shouldn't it have been obvious from my face that I was THE AUTHOR? I felt strange at work, too, and though I tried to hide it, I knew my colleagues looked at me differently. I would go to the office coffee machine with an insufferable half-smile, greeting everyone with ridiculous complacency: after all, I was the author of *Inventario* and they weren't.

Ultimately, I realized that no one—except of course the critics who treated me worst—cared that I was THE AUTHOR of whatever. A bigger stir was caused when I first appeared with a pregnant belly. Such excitement! Such commotion! Everyone wanted to touch the bump, ask about the baby's sex, which names we were considering. They went so far as to offer suggestions.

I suppose the brouhaha was a consequence of our country's abysmal birth rate. Books, in contrast, reproduce uncontrollably: they are a plague.

A few months later, having become, by that point, a mother, everything had changed. When I went out without the baby—a rare occurrence—I felt very differently than I had with the book. No smug half smile. By contrast, I felt naked, incomplete, an unwitting fraud. I felt I should explain myself to everyone who passed me on the street: hey, wait a minute, this isn't me, something is missing, don't you see? I'm a mother. I know I'm alone right now, but this isn't me, you don't understand.

Sometimes, I did feel like I needed to be free of the baby. But every time I went for a walk by myself, the sense that I was still carrying him around in my conscience was even worse.

After three months with no more than three hours of sleep in a row, after the home nursing visits to check the newborn's weight—weekly, at first, then every fifteen days—after an exhaustive tallying of the baby's excrement, vomit, boogers, and coughs, my identity as a mother had devoured all other identities and banished all my other selves into exile. Me, a writer? Me, a worker? Me, a wife? Me, a daughter? Me, a woman who had frolicked naked in the fountain in Trafalgar Square? Me, the woman who was a summer tour guide at Loch Ness and used it to hook up with American tourists? Impossible, simply impossible.

The phone call from the Basque Government made it clear to me: I was no longer myself. And once the initial daze wore off, I made a decision. It was time to turn things around; somehow, I had to start piecing back together my essential self, picking up the crumbs wherever they lay. And to undertake a challenge of such magnitude, I knew of only one path.

I let a couple of days go by before cluing in Niclas to my decision; I didn't want him to think that it was a childish impulse. We celebrated the news of the prize. I even allowed myself a bit of cava, chased by some nursing mother's guilt. I sensed Niclas was surprised by my enthusiasm. It was a prize, okay, it was a good prize, and came with good money, but not so much that it would change my life. In our home, bath time tended to be the most relaxed part of the evening for all three of us, and so that's when I chose to tell him: with the prize money, with those eighteen thousand euros ("minus taxes," he had to add, always sensitive to financial constraints), I was thinking about taking leave starting in February.

February 1st, the date circled in red on both our calendars. It was my last day of maternity leave, plus the leave hours I'd accrued for breastfeeding, plus all my vacation time for the year, and we were entering unknown territory: it was our duty to return to civic life, me and the scar between my legs, as if nothing had happened.

Niclas's eyes lit up. He was as worried as I was—if not more—about sending the baby to daycare at only six months old. That doesn't happen in Sweden. He thought it was a stupendous idea, of course. In fact, he had been weighing the possibility himself, although he hadn't dared to bring it up. And, on second thought, he could take leave himself; after all, me going back to work wouldn't be a bad thing, he knew that the months of maternal isolation had been hard on me. I had to cut off his musings straightaway:

"No, Niclas. I'll be the one taking leave. And Erik will go to daycare in February." He had the bewildered look of someone experiencing an acute attack of lost-in-translation. "I'm going on leave. To write."

As a citizen of the most feminist country on the planet (that's how they liked to be recognized), Niclas said nothing, but went pale. And he was still pale when, once the baby was asleep, we sat down to dinner. I tried to soften the blow. For him, and for me.

"It'll just be for four hours, from nine to one. Not the seven we'd planned on. He already naps in the morning, he won't even notice."

I rambled on in a rush about the daycare, the good impression we'd gotten from the open house, about Montessori and Pickler, and all those super-respectful techniques they used with the kids. He said he understood; he had never been an obstacle to my literary career and he wouldn't be this time either. For a moment I was afraid he was going to bring up the fascinating New Jersey vacation we'd taken when I was researching my book. Fortunately, he didn't mention New Jersey.

It's not easy being a writer's partner. It's nobody's choice: it happens to you. Niclas finished his omelet and drank the last sip of beer, then asked:

"So, what are you going to write about? Do you have something in mind?"

I spoke with deliberate calm. I didn't want him to sense my anxiety, the urgency and obsession in my words.

"I'll probably write something about that woman who killed her kids last summer—you remember?"

Monthly finances for a *materfamilias*:
√ Rent: 730 euros
√ Electricity: 55 euros
√ Gas: 90 euros
√ Phone and internet: 90 euros
√ Daycare: 190 euros
√ Food and sundries: 300 euros
√ Diapers (generic brand): 80 euros
√ Car expenses: 150 euros
√ Various streaming and media subscriptions: 40 euros
√ Ongoing donations to nonprofits: 50 euros
√ Other expenses (always cropping up): 200 euros

A total of 1,975 euros, every month. All of a sudden it seemed like a terrible number, uncontrollable, impossible to reduce except to the detriment of Palestinian refugees. Niclas earned 1,200 euros from the language school, so this meant that every month I needed to add 775 euros just to maintain a lifestyle that, aside from the baby's organic cereal, did not include any luxuries.

I didn't mention my project at work. Officially, I was a good mother who took additional leave in order to care for her child. Seemingly, I wasn't inconveniencing anyone. My boss reassured me again how, from an HR standpoint, it was a lot harder to square going down to part-time compared to a full leave. I signed the necessary paperwork, let them touch Erik, whom I paraded through the office tucked in the baby carrier, and left there a free woman. Or as free a woman as a mother can be.

I still had one test to overcome. I still had to leave the baby at daycare. At that point we began what is known as the *period of adaptation*, which consists of resisting the temptation to throw the baby directly into the pool and instead let him dip his toes in the water, get acclimated, go a little deeper, up to his knees, etc. On the first day, I stayed with him in the classroom. On the second, I went out into the hallway, leaving him alone for twenty minutes. On the third day, I managed to escape to the café across the street for a full forty-five minutes. From the fourth day on, I decided to bring my laptop. Erik rode in the baby carrier in front, my computer in the backpack on my back.

By the time the majority of the mothers (and the occasional father) left the daycare, holding back tears, I would already be sitting in the café waiting for Windows to boot. Sometimes a group of mothers who had met thanks to their kids and enjoyed a kind of social life together as a result sat at the table next to mine. They looked at me with curiosity. I tried to ignore them: I couldn't afford to waste a single minute.

During the two weeks of Erik's adaptation, I laid the ground-work for my future investigation. I made lists, identified primary sources, decided my approach for Jade/Alice's story, determined the places I would visit, debated what authority I could claim. Would I be a lawyer for the defense, or did my role need to be closer to that of prosecutor? What did I want? Was it the writer's legitimate obligation to be judge? Or did that onus fall to readers? Was I justified in making use of fiction, or should I stick to the facts and leave in everything we couldn't know or even intuit in the penumbra? And if I ruled out a more journalistic style, what were my options? How could I possibly stylize violence perpetrated against children? The question made me shudder. I decided to ignore it for the time being.

What should I do, for instance, with the dates, names, specific details? Change them for moral reasons? Legal ones? Literary? And the thing that had been needling me from the beginning: should I get in touch with Jade/Alice? Would it be appropriate to write her a letter, as that famous French writer had done with the guy who murdered his own wife and kids? And what about a face-to-face meeting? Setting aside my own inclinations (which were mixed, and therefore didn't help), I wondered if—in literary terms—the work lent itself to such an encounter, or whether a meeting with the accused would contaminate the book, diverting the focus away from what really mattered? If a tête-à-tête were possible—which I doubted—how much did I have to gain, and how much to lose?

These were the kinds of lists, concerns, questions I compulsively typed while Erik was adapting to daycare. Resigning himself, more likely.

I still received the odd phone call from local publications and radio stations—the tail-end of the hype that had come with the prize—which always made me lose my concentration. Later, when the mothers at the next table stood up, I imitated them, closing my computer, washing my hands, and running to cover my brave little Viking in kisses and hugs before putting him in the baby carrier and bringing him home.

I still feel nostalgia for those early days, when the book was nothing but a promise, shiny and colossal.

3.

NATURAL KILLERS

Houses belong to the neighbors
Countries, to foreigners
Children belong to the women
who never wanted children.

ANA MARTINS MARQUES

The clinic is located off the highway that connects Erandio with Sopelana, on the right if you're driving toward the coast. Gridlock is more common than not in that area, but you can always find parking behind the clinic. The building looks new with its pristine glass-plate façade. The sign advertising the services offered by the clinic goes virtually unnoticed by drivers.

This is where it all began.

Ritxi and Alice came here on twenty-two occasions. From the first concerns to the final victory. A pilgrimage lasting two and a half years. They turned those doctor appointments into day trips, to keep their spirits up. Ritxi was better at this: his optimism knew no bounds. At the clinic he was docile, an obedient patient.

Alice's mood changed by the day. Sometimes she seemed on top of the world, sometimes down in the dumps. She never found even ground. In general, she wasn't much for talking.

If Ritxi's schedule allowed, after the appointment they'd take the rest of the day off and go somewhere special for lunch. When the weather was nice, they drove out to Pobeña or the Old Port in Algorta. In the winter, they would go to Bilbao. They both loved the restaurant awarded a Michelin star on the Marzana pier: Alice wasn't a drinker and she tried to eat as cleanly as possible, and there they could always find a dish appropriate for her pre-pregnant condition.

They'd heard that alarm bells should go off if there was no success after a year of trying the old-fashioned way. They didn't even wait that long. Ritxi felt he was getting old; there was a smothering sense of urgency. He wasn't used to losing. After seven barren months, and in hopes of not delaying parenthood any longer, they resorted instead to a highly recommended clinic.

So, this where it all began. In this pastel-colored waiting room. The bloodwork and the spermiograms, the karyotype analysis, the ultrasounds, the primrose oil and folic acid, the monitoring of those hormones that cower behind unintelligible abbreviations (FSH, LT, AMH), the gynecologist, endocrinologist, hematologist, the hysterosalpingography, the white coats, the blue scrubs. This is where they received the first vague diagnosis (low ovarian reserve), the first treatment (Gonal and Ovitrelle), the antral follicle count, and the final intervention: artificial insemination.

Those pastel waiting room walls, again and again. Copies of magazines that were only sporadically updated. The fellow pilgrims waiting in the other chairs suddenly transformed into contenders for the prize: who will get there first? you? me? them? Who will never get there? Elbows thrown, telepathic tripping, dirty play. In short, open competition.

According to the marketing for assisted reproduction clinics, they are offering clients a service: they meet a clinical, scientific, practical demand. You want something (a blond baby) and, if you leave yourself in their hands, that's what you'll get (a 90-percent success rate, if the advertising is true). Is there anything this phase of late capitalism can't deliver? Our material and spiritual needs, the marketplace has them covered. So then why not the need to reproduce, which lands in a gray area somewhere between the two? You want to do this? You can! Not without a struggle, of course. The choice is yours: fight for it or shut up. Who likes a crybaby? Nobody. Okay then.

Neoliberal language is emotional, inspiring, empowering. And corrupt.

It converts desires into rights and rights into desires. Lie down, spread your legs. Concentrate on your dreams: if you wish really hard, they'll come true.

Oh dear, it looks like you didn't wish hard enough. The first attempt is a failure. You've spent the past two weeks afraid to make sudden movements, you've sworn off ham, avoided beer like the plague. But now here's your period. Rotten, repugnant blood. Defeat.

Would you like to speak with our psychologist? She can see you this coming Monday. She'll help you pick up the shattered pieces of your stymied hope so you can start over with positive energy and renewed strength. What's more, now you know what you can expect along the way: you've felt the pain (the shots in your abdomen, the bruising), you're familiar with the once indecipherable jargon (recombinant gonadotropin, estradiol, antral follicles), you already know how to cope with the guilt (you know it's not your fault, you can frame it in terms of unfairness: why her and not me?).

And then there are the people around you. This time you know it's better not to share too much. People who use three kinds of birth control and still end up pregnant. Those people. People who say don't obsess, just relax and enjoy yourself, hey, maybe all you need is a great lay (ha ha ha), come on girl, it'll happen when you least expect it, you'll see, just like what happened to this guy at work's cousin, etc.

People. Don't talk to people. Better to stay quiet.

Look at your partner. Hold his hand. Console each other. How could you have ever expected something like this? In the beginning, God created Heaven and Earth. Then he created Man and Woman, and he blessed them: Be fruitful, and multiply, and replenish the Earth. He said nothing about artificial insemination, nothing about Gonal or Ovitrelle. Not one word about recombinant fucking gonadotropin.

Couples don't always come out stronger from these situations. If the man is the problem—which is almost always the case— his sense of masculinity may suffer: problems with self-esteem, shame, a violent reaction—all common. If it's the woman, often- times she's tormented by the idea that her partner will leave her: *Why would he stay with me when he can find someone more fertile?* Not for nothing, but misogynistic cultures—i.e., all cultures— consider infertility to be grounds for abandoning a woman. Or for bringing a concubine into the home. When she found she couldn't conceive, Jacob's wife, Rachel, offered her husband the body of her own slave, Bilha, so he could at least have progeny. And progeny he had: old Jacob wasn't one for keeping idle.

Even if the most cutting-edge clinics guarantee a success rate of 90 percent, one out of every ten uteruses yearning to gestate and give birth are still unable to do so. This is the danger that always lies in wait, always weighs heavily. But the fight must go on. Who likes losers, whiners, weaklings?

I'm sorry to press, but have we gone over our flexible financing options?

When I'm finally out of the waiting room—having been politely shown the door after stating what I wanted—I realize the shortcomings of my approach. I wrote the lines above as if Alice/ Jade was a run-of-the-mill mother who had trouble conceiving, a typical female with a typical desire to hold her own little one in her arms. And maybe that's the wrong tack. But I still don't know what I need, except to keep searching. This is why I'm at the clinic, spying on these candidates vying for fatherhood, for motherhood. Why I make a brazen but futile attempt to speak to the doctors. And it's why, when she sees me in the cafeteria with only my chicken-scratch notebook for company, the chubby woman from reception takes pity on me. Luckily, she's a professional gossip. She remembers Alice, of course. How could she not, Alice is taboo around here, no one mentions her name but everybody remembers the couple's long course of treatment. Like me, the receptionist isn't sure whether or not I should consider Alice as just another patient. They did at the clinic, of course. But she was a woman of extremes, that Alice. Sometimes she was on top of the world, sometimes she was down in the dumps. Never on even ground. This is all she tells me.

In any case, since there was still no pregnancy after three cycles of insemination—all multiplied by three, the injections, the ultrasounds, the follicle count—it was recommended that Ritxi and Alice take the next step: in vitro fertilization, life from a test tube. A longer process, and more expensive, painful, and distressing than insemination. They said yes, of course. They were long past the point of no return.

Here's a working hypothesis: maybe she didn't want children and that's why she didn't get pregnant naturally; maybe she was secretly on the pill, or used a clandestine diaphragm, or tracked her fertile days and sneakily avoided sex. Maybe the mere aversion to motherhood prevented pregnancy (the inverse of having faith in the powers of the conscious mind: *enjoy, don't obsess, when you least expect it*). Maybe she went to the first consultation thinking it would just be a one-time thing, make the man happy, etc., only to see herself forced down a tunnel she didn't know how to get out of. Maybe she didn't inject the Gonal correctly, maybe she reduced the dose with a few discreet twists of the injection pen; maybe, when she was alone in the room after each insemination, she didn't follow the recommendation to try to have an orgasm, maybe instead she placed her hands on her abdomen and begged, implored the sperm to veer off track *for the love of God*.

Pure speculation. Maybe she did everything expected of a woman. Maybe she was like Hannah in the Old Testament who, when she knew she couldn't beget children, knelt before God and prayed: *Lord Almighty, if you will indeed look upon the affliction of your maidservant and remember me, if you will not forget me and will give me a male child, then I will give him unto you all the days of his life, and no razor shall touch his head.* Perhaps this could be our approach: all Alice wanted was her own blond baby and she was willing to make whatever sacrifice she could from the very beginning. And until the end.

I've tried to empathize with the candidates for motherhood in this waiting room. Understand their hopes and frustrations, even though I had a very different experience. There was no primrose oil in my case, no grapefruit juice or folic acid, no monitoring my basal temp in the morning or keeping my legs in the air after ejaculation. My pregnancy was an unexpected shock. I sound like a brainless teenager if I explain exactly how it happened. When I used to hear couples over thirty say they'd gotten pregnant "by accident," I always had the suspicion that what they meant was "without talking about it," "having made a tacit decision," "letting Nature do her work without us explicitly planning the nature of our humping." And yet I can flat out say that it is perfectly possible for a stable, well-educated adult couple to have an unintended pregnancy. I won't go into detail, but let's just say that after trying the gamut of onerous birth control methods, we settled on one, never-recommended practice. This method worked for a year until, once we were lulled into complacency, it proved the warning "it always sprinkles before it rains."

I went to the pharmacy on the fourth day of my missed period, mostly to rule out the remote possibility of a pregnancy as early as possible. And yet, when faced with the urine-damp stick proclaiming "YES," I proved to be more incredulous than afraid.

I wanted children (I wanted children?) in an abstract, general way. I had been telling myself that I still had a margin of four or five years to make that abstraction tangible. Anyhow, the timing wasn't right. Not only had I finally managed to finish and publish a book, but that book had brought me a certain amount of success that I was enjoying at the moment. I spent my youth turning my back on my true vocation for reasons accessible only to an experienced psychoanalyst. But since I'd moved into my thirties, I had found a locus, an energy, an endless source of satisfaction in writing. Through it, I'd gone from skulking around the edges of my proper place—so close that I could hear the other writers' laughter and sighs through the wall—to occupying space at the center of where I belonged. And ostensibly, that was the future I could expect: more books, more readers, a life dedicated to matters existing beyond the spectrum of what we can see. I'm not talking about vanity, prizes, or praise. I'm talking about what comes before and after all that. A new kind of clarity, an anchor that grounds you without weighing you down, a pouring forth that comes directly from the stomach, a gut feeling so potent that it drives you to fill pages and pages with black marks. That's what I'm talking about. In this new configuration of the world, I didn't need babies.

And then there was the question of Niclas. Friend, lover, a good and decent guy, reliable and polite, blonde and blue-eyed, though not necessarily handsome. Niclas. Was he the one destined to be the father of my children? I wasn't sure. Could I imagine him in the delivery room, murmuring words of encouragement in my ear? Absolutely not. Although I couldn't imagine myself in that situation, either. But no, I had never thought about Niclas as a father.

Maybe, like in the fantasies my high school friends and I shared, I saw myself instead as a single mother, with my daughter always by my side, the two of us against the world, whatever happened.

That wasn't it either.

If I stop and categorize the types of relationships I've had in this life, I find, on the one hand, tales of intoxicating love that only made me suffer, and on the other, lukewarm relationships, comfortable and pleasant. Something told me I would eventually find the Holy Grail: intoxication without suffering, well-being without tepidness.

Instead, I was with Niclas, the most recent specimen from Group Two. Moreover, our survival as a couple depended on him always conforming to my whims and fluctuations. It appeared to be the natural order of things: he gave, I received. He left his job—when we met, Niclas was a well-paid and better-exploited worker in London—when I decided to return to the land of my birth. It took a lot of effort, but he finally managed to adapt to this disagreeable city, to a job he is overqualified for, to a laughable salary. And yet, it turns out one can still be ungrateful to a person who gives you everything.

At first, I blamed the pregnancy on Niclas and silently resented him for a few days. It was his fault, I knew he wanted to be a father, he took an interest in things I'd never heard of (Maxi-Cosi, transitional objects) because he'd known they'd be part of his near future, etc. Yet despite the initial shock and doubts that followed, once the first, faltering days had passed, I began to embrace my new responsibility—the ineludible mission of motherhood. I even began to *want* that future baby, once I'd ruled out Niclas's guilt in a pregnancy plot.

And naturally, I learned what a Maxi-Cosi was.

And lots of other new words, virtually all of them unpleasant: *meconium, lanugo, amniocentesis, progesterone, vernix, prodromal labor, colostrum.* I'm convinced that women will never have full-fledged control of our pregnancy and labor until we reconstruct the dictionary. With such a horrendous lexical web—suggesting both terminal illness and biblical curse in equal measure—it is absolutely impossible to feel like the heroine of our gestation odyssey or to be conscious of the magnitude of the change we are about to experience. I humbly propose that we inspire ourselves in the nautical dictionary instead: *abyssal, voyage, schooner, mistral, anchor, journey* . . . now that's more like it, for goodness' sake!

I really shouldn't complain. At least I didn't have to learn about follicle counts, natural killer cells that protect the mother but attack the fetus, anti-Müllerian hormone, heparin injections to prevent miscarriage, all those things women with fertility problems learn the hard way. Until recently, I didn't even know they existed. For me, pregnancy had been a latent menace, a skilled sharpshooter ready to end my life as I liked it.

Maybe that's how Alice saw it, as well. And in that elegant clinic, amid those pastel colors, she was left at the mercy of a squad of white coats with no chance of defending herself.

The pregnancy was confirmed by a blood test. I imagine the couple's cautious happiness. Ritxi would provide the happiness, and Alice the caution. Following the patients' wishes, two embryos had been transferred and another three were frozen. The quality of those embryos (Grade B) suggested that the probability of a twin pregnancy was "medium." Ritxi didn't like the word *medium.* They were told about the risks of carrying multiples: preeclampsia, growth restriction, premature labor, C-section, etc. Even so, they wanted both. Two aces up their sleeve. A few days later, they learned via sonogram that both embryos were viable.

I had no news about what was cooking inside of me until my twelve-week ultrasound, and I remember my relief when I saw on the screen that there was only going to be one. Niclas's first words when we left the clinic, however, were, "Just one, what a shame!"

4.

FORENSIC MEDICINE

O love, how did you get here?
O embryo
Remembering, even in sleep,
Your crossed position.

SYLVIA PLATH

They are acts constituting a criminal offense. Acts committed with criminal intent, subject to definition in accordance with the law. "The acts," words that serve as a euphemism for the incident at the heart of a trial, or allow us to avoid naming the incident altogether, given that until the trial is over, the incident itself isn't quite made of solid stuff. The letters *A-C-T* conceal the act itself. Until proven, it doesn't exist. I'll also use the term. The acts. Frankly, *homicide*, *infanticide*, *murder*, *double drowning* prove unbearable to write: they cling to my fingertips, they hang, suspended, over the keyboard. They don't dare make the jump.

In November of the year the acts were committed, I took advantage of my trip to Vitoria to accept the Euskadi Prize to see the Armentia neighborhood for the first time. Niclas swapped his afternoon classes with a colleague and we went as a family to accept the award. My father would come a little later, on his own. My mother was incapable of finding a reasonably priced plane ticket; apparently, November is a busy month (the first I'd heard of it). I told her not to worry, it was just a formality. We would celebrate the next time she came to visit.

The weather was awful, rain sweeping across the highway and rattling the trees. Still, with only an hour to go before the ceremony, I convinced Niclas to make a quick stop in Vitoria's wealthiest neighborhood. Finding a place to park was easy, as was locating the house, which had been thoroughly photographed in the days following the incident. The chalet rose elegantly from the edge of a field beside the lovely Roman basilica—a popular pilgrimage site—and at a palatable distance from the other homes. Assertive and symmetrical, the house stood proudly under the rain as if nothing of note had occurred within its walls, as if everything had gone just as the builders had planned. The entire façade of the second floor was a giant glass window, now hidden behind gray exterior blinds. The rest of the structure looked like a traditional Basque farmhouse: pitched roof, exposed timber.

Although the house was shuttered and empty, someone had been making sure the yard was kept maintained. Maybe it was on the market, a reasonable assumption, even with no visible "for sale" sign. In Hong Kong, they use the word *hongza* to describe homes that are silent witnesses to suicide or violent crimes. Their value tends to plummet, making them attractive properties for investors confident of the short memory spans of home buyers. In Japan, they are the *jiko bukken*, "marked" homes you can search for specifically, using a filter on real estate websites. The morbid details are included. Who, how, when.

Two babies, drowned in the bathtub, the height of summer.

The acts.

Did I sense something as I stood there, in front of the house? A slight vibration? An air of doom, of foreboding? I thought so, but Niclas disagreed: it was November, that was all, night was falling, it was pouring rain. The baby was asleep in the carrier and a single umbrella couldn't protect all three of us. Niclas was obviously uneasy there—who wouldn't be? What did the neighbors, who were few and far between, do when they walked past it? Did they bring visitors, linger out front, embellish their tour with sinister details? Or had it become the neighborhood's big taboo, like in the fertility clinic? An incident to conceal, hushed and forgotten, for the good of the local reputation and property values?

We didn't see anyone else, so I can only speculate.

I made a few notes once we were back in the car and on our way to the presidential seat of the Basque Government. Engrossed, I didn't notice that the rain had completely plastered my hair to my head. Pictures from the ceremony clearly show I hadn't looked in a mirror before stepping on stage to accept the award from the Basque President. Plenty of Twitter comments were made about my appearance, along with suggestions that I'd only gotten the award because I was a girl.

The first days are clear-cut. Well-documented. Just as they must be in a well-directed court case. I'm not sure whether such a profusion of details is an advantage or an impediment to the search for the whole story.

The authorities never considered alternative suspects. There hadn't been any trace of someone else in the house, and the home security cameras didn't register any motion in the four hours between when the au pair left and when she returned. No wolves, no dingoes. The hypothesis of accidental death was automatically ruled out, due to the statistical impossibility of two identical accidents occurring successively. The media, however, did insinuate that the first death could have been a case of involuntary manslaughter, and that the mother—overwhelmed by the situation, in a grievous state of shock—then committed the second murder. Pure speculation. From the point of view of the forensic investigators, the case was simple. All evidence and reports were sent to the judge posthaste.

After doing away with her little ones, Alice was taken into police custody and brought to the hospital in Santiago, to the seventh floor—a habitual refuge of anorexics and alcoholics. The psychiatrists on duty noted that they found Alice "disoriented and in a state of shock," leaving open the possibility of "dissociative amnesia." They gave her sedatives. She barely spoke, although on several occasions they heard her whisper "where are they?" and "they're all right now, aren't they?" When asked what her name was, Alice told them "Jade," which confused the doctors. Officers were posted outside her room the whole time. Forensic investigators had already collected her clothes and immediately sealed them in plastic evidence bags. Her hands were swabbed for biological evidence.

It was very late by the time she was finally allowed to sleep.

The next morning, medical examiners sent by the investigating judge arrived at the hospital to perform tests on the patient. Alice was examined over the course of three hours, while a new set of officers guarded the door. Though she had refused breakfast, Alice was beginning to show some signs of awareness. She asked about her children, and when they told her what had happened, she shouted that it wasn't possible; "Never never never," she screamed and wailed. Eventually, her howling faded to a dull moan. Then came silence, and soon after, more shaking, more spasms.

A public defender also turned up at the hospital that morning. He had a gentle way about him and a youthful appearance, and had just spent half the night at the police station helping a kid under arrest for assaulting a supermarket security guard. Now he found himself in the midst of a situation unparalleled in the eight years he had worked in legal aid. He hadn't slept in twenty-six hours and, faced with the stifling heat and a broken client, he struggled to get control of the situation. The young lawyer finally had the presence of mind to advise his client of her right to choose not to testify before the judge. It seemed that Alice heard him and even followed his advice, since the judge got nothing from Alice but tears and a few final exhausted sobs when he arrived at the hospital.

By that time, the consequences of the acts—the two small bodies, in other words—were already in the Basque Institute of Legal Medicine on Avenida Gasteiz, awaiting autopsy. An autopsy that would reveal no surprises. The same cause of death: drowning. Foam in the lungs, water in the stomach, the left cavity of the heart drained of blood. Those little hearts left no room for other hypotheses. The very next day, the investigating judge wrote the order for Alice's incarceration and she was sent to the prison in Zaballa, a prescription for sleeping pills and sedatives in hand. No one was certain that she was even aware of the crimes. The media disseminated all manner of opinions: "Not even an eternity in Hell could atone for what she's done, that vile woman," a very concerned male citizen of Vitoria declared. Another citizen, a woman this time, and if possible even more upset, expressed another view: "The real punishment will come once she realizes what she's done, wretched woman."

Alice spent five days total in prison, all of them in the infirmary, since no one really knew what to do with her or which protocols to follow. Prisons were not built for women like Alice.

Ritxi didn't return to the house in Armentia after the first interrogation. It was reported that a friend picked him up at the station and took him straight to his house in Elciego. Only one newspaper bothered to mention this; as for the others, Ritxi was absent. How he spent those five days or what might have gone through his head will forever remain a mystery.

Over the course of the five days Alice spent behind bars, three notable things occurred. Although it was expected, the first thing was still horrible. The other two were completely unanticipated.

First, the twins were cremated at a funeral facility on the outskirts of Vitoria. It was an intimate event: Ritxi, his brother, who had recently arrived from Austin, and a few close friends. They took a car to and from the facility. There are no pictures from inside the funeral home. I don't know if they read poems or sang something during the service. It's better this way. Who wants to know those details? Not even I do.

Second, despite the fact that they'd adopted a different strategy in the first days following the crimes, the media suddenly began to show sympathy for Alice. Reviewing documentation in the archives from a certain distance, as I do now, the change in how the press painted her is certainly striking. Alice was declared broken, incapable of accepting what she had done. It was argued that the very act of committing the crimes would have been torture, that she would never get over it, that the rest of her life would be perpetual Hell. The possibility of postpartum depression was raised, suggested for the first time by a neighbor—a supposed neighbor, I've never been able to locate her—and later in the form of assumptions, percentages, and symptoms bandied about by psychiatric experts. It's possible that the media employed this new framework with the simple, honest goal of milking the public's interest in the story. The origins of media conspiracies are often rather dull.

Who knows. In any case, public opinion liked the new angle. It meant people could abandon the crude terrain of crime reporting, the banal territory of *the acts*, of what happened, and become fully immersed in the heart of a modern-day Greek tragedy.

And lastly, there is the most surprising detail, the thing I have the most trouble understanding: Ritxi decided to hire Alice a good lawyer.

The day after his children were cremated, Ritxi momentarily broke his self-exile in the Rioja Alavesa to get in touch with his personal lawyer and ask for the name of the best criminal defense lawyer in the city. A female attorney, close to retirement and with a reputation as a feminist activist, came up immediately: Carmela Basaguren. She agreed to take the case the same day they contacted her and got right to work. At the time, the priority was getting Alice out of the jail in Zaballa. A motion to this effect came swiftly across the judge's desk. The document, well-constructed and convincing, detailed the reasons Alice should be released from pre-trial detention: the impossibility of committing the same crime again, roots in the community, lack of flight risk, etc., etc.

In their arguments, Alice's defense gave early indication that they expected an acquittal on the grounds of extenuating circumstances due to mental derangement. The criminal code had foreseen these situations: Article 20.1, specifically, establishes that an individual "who, due to any psychiatric anomaly or alteration at the time the crime is committed, is unable to understand the illegality of the act, or act in accordance with this understanding" is absolved of criminal responsibility, as Carmela Basaguren saw fit to remind the investigating judge, citing the statute word-for-word.

The prosecution couldn't have disagreed more and opposed Alice's release, citing the sheer seriousness of the case, as well as the charges against her: she was accused of two murders, a grievous crime multiplied by two, in addition to the aggravating circumstance of the family relationship. She was facing forty years in prison. But to the surprise of most observers, the judge ruled in support of the defense's request. With the seizure of her passport, an obligation to appear in court every fifteen days, and bail set at fifty thousand euros, Alice was released.

Free the murderess. Free the ghost.

There is a myth rooted in pre-Hispanic cultures that later gained strength during the colonial period. La Llorona, a woman who throws her two children (or son, or daughter, depending on the story) into a river. Devastated by guilt, she then kills herself and her ghost begins its erratic roaming, never straying far from bodies of water.

From Mexico to Chile, the story unfolds in similar ways; the mythemes (those small interchangeable puzzle pieces from which myths are constructed) are repeated. The modus operandi is almost always the same: the children are drowned (whether in a river or a lake), although sometimes stabbing is mentioned. In some places, such as Panama, the mother's negligence causes her child's death (the mother wants to dance, to go off and enjoy herself, and it occurs to her that by leaving the baby on a riverbank she can do so). But in most of the stories, the woman is seduced, impregnated, and later abandoned by the impregnator. And in these circumstances, without the means of survival for herself or her baby, she commits infanticide. There are also Lloronas who act out of spite, Hispanic Medeas who, with the intention of wounding the man who has abandoned them, decide to murder his offspring, the tangible fruit of a now-extinguished love.

In any case, the consequences are always the same: an errant soul, eternal punishment, infinite tears adding water to water.

That night, I dreamed of Australia. Despite systematically disregarding my dreams for decades, I feel the need to record this oneiric episode for future analysis. I don't really remember much: the arid Australian landscape, the whiff of threat, only vaguely sensed. The amorphous dream-memory didn't leave me over the course of the day, so I looked back over what I had written the previous day. I reread three or four pages and there I find it, that exotic word: dingo. What is a dingo, exactly? A wild dog, native to Southeast Asia but commonly found in Australia. *Canis lupus dingo*. But what is a dingo doing in my manuscript? I search for the word and don't have to wait long for an answer. It all comes back to me, images from a TV movie I saw as a child.

August 17th, 1980, in the vicinity of Ayers Rock, known today as Mount Uluru, sacred land in the North Territory in the center of Australia. It's here that the Chamberlain family were camping with their three children. While they barbecue their dinner, the youngest Chamberlain—Azaria, just nine weeks old—is left sleeping peacefully in the tent. In the middle of the meal, Lindy, the mother, thinks she hears barking. No one else seems to hear it, but her instinct tells her something is wrong. She dives into the tent, fearing the worst, and finds it empty: there is no trace of the newborn. In the midst of her terror, Lindy is able to glimpse the shape of a dingo disappearing into the darkness. Only the mother witnessed the animal, the rest of the family simply heard her screams. Azaria was never seen again.

The case could have wound up like so many other tragic accidents, becoming part of the fabric of popular culture, the moral of a story, a warning for negligent parents. But things didn't stop there. After twists and turns in the investigation and with a parallel, full-blown media trial raging in the Australian press, Lindy was ultimately sentenced to life in prison for the murder of her own daughter. What was the evidence pointing to such a crime? There wasn't much. The body was never found. There was never an indication that the mother had a motive. A pair of supposedly blood-stained scissors, conveniently exhibited to the public, turned out to just be covered in red paint. But the mother's attitude during the trial—cold, detached—was enough for a conscientious jury to send her to prison for the rest of her life.

Lindy gave birth to a fourth baby during her first weeks in jail. She spent three years behind bars before the case was reopened on account of new evidence: remnants of Azaria's clothing, found by a dingo lair. The discovery put the verdict in doubt and she was eventually released. Even so, the case wasn't closed definitively until 2012, when Azaria's death certificate was amended to indicate dingo attack as the cause of death. For her wrongful conviction, Lindy Chamberlain received a sizable settlement from the Australian government.

Who knows who let me watch the movie version of Azaria's case. I suppose it must have been my father, since I used to spend my weekends with him, watching TV in the afternoon while he dozed off beside me on the couch. What *wouldn't* I discover on those interminable Saturday and Sunday afternoons? How many monsters would come to inhabit my nightmares thanks to those movies? Fu Manchu, killer sharks, roaring crowds, Marisol and her lottery . . . Back then, I didn't know that Lindy Chamberlain was a real person and that her case was—is—the most famous crime in Australia. But clearly, the story left its mark; I still vaguely recalled it. And the word *dingo*, so chirpy-sounding on its own, still poisons my dreams.

Uluru.

Dingo.

Uluru.

Dingo.

Two pleasant words, lively, appealing, fitting for the title of a successful novel. Typographical oddity included.

I've combed through the archives, nosed around the lawyers' social media accounts, diligently read the penal codes—those currently in effect as well as previous versions—and browsed the forums where desperate citizens beg for legal assistance. Hours of conscientious work, and I'm rewarded with a sense that nothing could escape my notice. What occurred in the hours following the discovery is clear-cut. Crystal clear, too, are the standard police procedures, the good forensic practices, the steps taken by the investigating judge. Even Ritxi's behavior seems logical, easy to comprehend: his need to flee the spotlight, seek refuge with a friend, his state of shock, the denial phase, that choreography of grief so magnificently detailed in psychology manuals.

But after a certain point, things start to get murky. Then suddenly, I'm in the dark. No manual, no official document can guide me out of here. What should I do? Which path do I take?

Something changed in Ritxi after he said goodbye to his twins. This is where I start to lose my bearings. No one would have been surprised had Ritxi allied himself with the prosecution, if he had hired a lawyer guaranteed to get Alice the maximum sentence (the same lawyer he wound up hiring for the opposite purpose, perhaps); he was the crime's third victim after all. Instead he chose to do everything he could to free his wife from prison. Why? Which grief manual helps explain such unforeseen behavior? Had he always planned on it, but taken several days to put it into motion? Was it love? Compassion? Denial? Complicity, if only of the moral sort? And what did he hope for the future? Was he able to imagine any kind of future at all? To start over from square one with his wife? A new life? Another city? Another round of in vitro, perhaps? Did he remember the frozen embryos awaiting their chance? And what did his closest circle of friends, or his brother, say to him? Did anyone advise him not to rush, to take it slowly, to think it through very carefully? And when he finally picked up Alice outside the jail, what did he say to her? What did they say to each other?

You are forgiven, Alice.

What I did is unforgivable, Ritxi.

We can fix this.

This can't be fixed.

I'll help you, Alice.

I don't deserve your help.

In such a dramatic situation, maybe melodrama isn't likely at all. Maybe something along these lines:

How are you? They feeding you okay? You look thin.

That's more like it. In any case, they stayed together, and together they left the city and settled in a little house in Elciego, close to Ritxi's work. They went to Vitoria every fifteen days to sign in with the court; Ritxi always accompanied his wife. The first few times, photographers were waiting for them, hoping to get a shot of the couple. Gradually, they stopped showing up. And every fifteen days Ritxi and Alice went to Barcelona, to see a famous psychiatrist. Alice started treatment for psychosis. She kept her pills in a small plastic case with compartments for each day. She resumed painting, occupational therapy.

There are no pictures of Alice from this period. The media forgot her. Everyone forgot her. The twins were ash; the couple was too.

There would have been good times, as well; I can imagine them. Falling in love, planning a future in which another person fits, skin to skin, breath to breath, understanding each other, not understanding each other but loving each other anyway, routines built together, an intimacy incomprehensible to anybody else, words, hairs, soft touches.

When Ritxi met Jade, she was already going by Alice. She was working as a model-slash-actress in the filming of a corporate video for a Bordeaux winery. Ritxi happened to be in the city as a guest, compliments of an association dedicated to the advancement of viticulture. I can imagine the initial flutter, which we flippantly call *falling in love*. Alice's beauty. The scent of power around Ritxi, pleasant and magnanimous, his expensive tie, nice hair, but youthful, happy. He was ten years her senior. He spoke perfect French and it was obvious that the world was his oyster. What else did Alice need at the time? A tale as old as time, nothing mysterious about it. Ritxi asked if she was free for dinner. Yes, I think so, she replied. Filming had wrapped, but the train she was supposed to take back to Avignon was cancelled due to a railroad strike. Alice would be spending the night in Bordeaux. In short, it worked out perfectly. Ritxi chose the restaurant, an ideal little bistro. And he chose the wine, of course, a 2001 Chateau Latour-Martillac, by no means the most expensive on the menu, which would have been excessive. Alice still didn't know the extent of Ritxi's wealth, though she was trying to work it out.

She barely tasted the wine. He told her that, after studying in Paris and Washington, he had taken over the family business, a small winery in the Rioja Alavesa. His father had been at the helm until his sudden death the year before. He had a brother who was a scientist and quite removed from the world of business. Ritxi also told her that the company had belonged to his family for five generations; his comment implied mandatory commitment to producing a sixth heir, or at least that's how Alice understood it. Ritxi made no mention of his recent attempts to diversify the family's holdings, his strategic investments in wind energy and boutique hotels. There would be time for all that. Alice talked, too, with increasing ease: she told him she was a vegetarian (though the truth was, she barely ate; Ritxi couldn't help but notice how she moved her food around her plate to give the impression that she was consuming at least some of her meal) and that she dreamed of being a painter, but in the meantime made money as a model. She said she hated Avignon, especially in the summer, the heat, the mosquitos. She didn't mention any family. It didn't take long for the residues of melancholy to materialize about her. She was alone in the world.

Overall, Ritxi considered her interesting enough. He accompanied the girl back to her modest little hotel on the Rue Bouffard. Alice shared a room with a colleague—another model-slash-actress from the agency. They kissed in the doorway after Ritxi had warned her—*Alice, I'm going to kiss you*—and then said good night. Ritxi didn't invite her to his hotel—much more elegant than hers—and Alice didn't ask, although she did imagine the freshly-ironed sheets and bubble bath. It was 2006, the world was already hyperconnected by then, and besides, they only lived a few hundred kilometers from each other with an irrelevant border between them: they would obviously see each other again.

I've gleaned all of this from an interview Ritxi gave to an online wine magazine, the only interview in which he talks with unusual candor about his private life. *I fell in love with my wife over the competition's wine* reads the headline, and he certainly sounds like a man in love. Here is someone who let down his guard for once. Conventional and predictable, middle-almost-high class, although he might not be taken for it. After all, he was the guy who eschewed golf and took off for the mountains with his seven-thousand-euro bike. The guy who, instead of spending his vacation in an overwater bungalow in the Maldives, traveled the Trans-Siberian railroad alone with just a backpack. He practiced yoga every morning and kept—at least until he got married—a tarantula in a terrarium. A 70s hard rock fan—Led Zeppelin, chiefly—he always felt a little out of place in business meetings, an imprecise feeling that faded as he watched the clouds out the window or drew intricate doodles on a sheet of paper. He dreamed of retiring early and dedicating himself to volunteer work: tutoring the children of immigrants, cleaning beaches of plastic debris.

In marketing circles, a sphere I'm well familiar with, executives like Ritxi are a dime a dozen. Tempered extravagance is a requirement on any résumé worth its salt. But in the more traditional business of wine, however, people were likely to talk about a character like Ritxi, even turn him into a minor legend, a worthy object of all sorts of gossip. Ritxi knew this, and that's why he chose Alice. Because he found her darkness, her aura of loneliness, her broken wings, her artistic talent that was never fully realized and which filled her with frustration and rage sufficiently unconventional. In that period, all his male friends—not to mention his female ones—were already married, and diversity of character was conspicuous in its absence. Identical master's degrees, duplicate vacations, a platter of increasingly picked-over conversation topics.

Alice wasn't like that, but she was a quick learner; she had an air of willingness to adapt to something new. Ritxi knew his choice would fatten his reputation and grease the wheels of the rumor mill, and he liked that. He decided to marry her the same day they met. He imagined storms, explosive reconciliations, a life devoted to moving from one extreme to the other, excruciating happiness, impenetrable to those observing it from the outside, envy, admiration, ignorance, tremors.

It was all a game to him. The foreign caprice of a man who was used to having it all. Hence his responsibility, his guilt.

Perhaps.

5.

FAMILY FRIENDLY

There is no more somber enemy of good art
than the pram in the hall.

CYRIL CONNOLLY

Much is said about the exhaustion motherhood entails; the
lack of sleep, the bags under the eyes. Still, almost no mention
is ever made of the hours of boredom that fill a mother's life.
I'm talking about the succession of gray, amorphous days during
which breastfeeding, changing diapers, trying to get the crying
baby to sleep, and then checking to make sure it's breathing take
up your life to the point of suffocating it. Meanwhile, time flows
ahead normally for the rest of humanity. Isolated, confined, and
absorbed twenty-four hours a day by a job that confers a social
status similar to cleaning toilets (and I say this with firsthand
knowledge, because there was a time during which I worked
cleaning toilets). Hours that drag by, gazes lost somewhere in the
distance. Always given over to the other. In a hypocritical society
that tells you that there's nothing more desirable, nothing more
revolutionary, than devoting yourself to the other, a silent riot in
the heart of the cost-benefit paradigm.

Okay, sure.

If it were really so beautiful, desirable, and revolutionary, then by now men would have taken it upon themselves to stay home and send women out to work; there's no doubt about that.

But I don't want to get too far off-track. You can complain about exhaustion, but not boredom. That's a frivolous complaint, incomprehensible; if you're bored, maybe you should have another child, or seven more, like our grandmothers did. Do you think they had time to be bored? Come on, grow up—you're a mother now.

If it doesn't rain, we take a walk: miles and miles in order to feel like you are master of your steps, push the stroller uphill and hang on to it going down. Suddenly, you're captivated by your own reflection in a store window. You look wilted, decayed. The baby cries because he prefers movement, he's unnerved by the interruption and again you have to start pushing, walking, moving forward, bouncing. It's worse if it rains. All you have left is to remember to look out the window once in a while, assure yourself that the world is still out there, the traffic light, red, green, red, umbrellas knocking into each other, it's all gray, until suddenly, a plastic grocery bag tears and a parade of oranges fills the sidewalk, a touch of color at last. Or when a call from a telemarketer is a memorable event—as long as it doesn't interrupt a nap—the novelty of the day or even the week, and you find yourself driven to respond enthusiastically to that voice, masculine and sweet, Caribbean, that explains in detail the advantages Jazztel offers in fiber-optic internet, mobile coverage, and ADSL, to the point that you comfortably call him by his first name, how interesting, Julio, that's not bad at all, I'll think it over, will you give me another call tomorrow, Julio?

Doris Lessing wrote: *There is nothing more boring for an intelligent woman than to spend endless amounts of time with small children.* I like this quote because it confirms that I am an intelligent woman. Somewhere else, Doris described motherhood as the Himalaya of Tedium. In Rhodesia, pregnant at the age of nineteen. And at twenty, pregnant again. Lessing's legend is intertwined with her volatile mothering: she abandoned John and Jean, the children from her first marriage, in Africa—what was then known as Southern Rhodesia—and went off to London with the fruit of her second marriage before divorcing for the second time. This third child, Peter, fragile and sickly from birth, died at sixty-six years old. Doris cared for him until the very end. The Nobel Prize winner herself would die a few weeks later. A whole life given to another, for ninety-four years.

But we should be clear. Sometimes, it can be something beautiful, desirable, revolutionary. At some point on our journey up the eight thousand steps of the Himalaya of Tedium, when we are shattered, almost out of oxygen, the match is struck, the spark ignites, a small flame illuminates the here and now, and a reverberating quake wins one ephemeral battle for eternity.

For example: you have the baby at your breast, like always, skin to skin, warmth to warmth, and suddenly you realize that nursing is no longer painful, his steady gnawing no longer hurts, it doesn't even bother you: in fact, it's actually starting to feel pleasant. The baby is focused on his inexhaustible ingesting and so are you. At last, you are free to submerge yourself in the bath of prolactin and its stupefying relaxation. You could fall asleep right there as the world dissolves, you dissolve, and the baby dissolves, you are one now, a unified everything dissolving in oxytocin. At that exact instant, the baby pulls away, milk drips from the corners of his mouth, nothing but abundance and satisfaction, and he looks you directly in the eyes; not only is he looking at you, you can feel that he *sees* you, and he smiles and you return his smile, pure love and mutual gratitude. And then you know that you have reached the peak of human sensuality, that nothing can compete with this moment, the sensation in your nipples, your limitless skin, the trickle of hot milk, the smile, the most honest of gazes.

I felt compassion for Niclas then, real compassion, because I knew he would never even get close to that feeling.

Another writer, another mother. The Scot Muriel Spark. She abandoned her child, as well. Also in Southern Rhodesia (what is up with Rhodesia, the bitch, the south). Poor Samuel Robin, left in the care of his manic-depressive father in Zimbabwe, when it was known as Southern Rhodesia. What if I include *Rhodesia* in the title of this book of mine?

Uluru.

Dingo.

Rhodesia.

The list grows longer still. I like it.

With the help of daycare, things started to change for the better. The pangs of guilt I felt when I dropped the baby off vanished as soon as I heard the first notes of Windows launching, to the degree that Erik's four hours of institutionalization flew by. I decided to stay and work on my laptop in the cafes close to the daycare, to save myself the roundtrip to and from the house. I tried to frequent various locales, since I tended to get dirty looks from the waitstaff when the hours passed and I was still sitting there in front of an empty coffee cup, eyes glued to my screen. I wrote with the same excitement as the old days, my body and soul working toward a common goal. I was building Alice while also rebuilding myself.

Unfortunately, the creative euphoria of those first days wasn't lasting. On the one hand, I was worn out. Erik was still waking up three or four times every night to feed. On the other, well . . . I don't know, I simply let the hours tick by, I sat at the bar and read the paper, initiated absurd Google searches. There were days when I didn't write a single new word. Other days when the only thing I accomplished was erasing some of the words I had written the day before. It had only been three months since the Euskadi Prize and I was still getting offers to do talks and book clubs, to judge contests. And I had to decline the vast majority of times, offering more excuses than were necessary: I was responsible for a baby, the father worked in the evenings, grandparents were absolutely no help, what else do you want me to say.

I would be frustrated when I returned to pick up Erik, even more irritated when I thought ahead to all the things I had to do next: prepare lunch, feed Erik, try to get him down for a nap, eat with Niclas while struggling to find any topic of conversation . . . and then once we'd cleaned everything up and Niclas had gone back to school, the baby would wake up while I was still in the middle of brushing my teeth. To Hell with my intention of getting in a five-minute nap on the couch. Then, weather permitting, we would go out for our walk and I would give him his snack on a bench beside the estuary. If not, we would stay at home, lying on a blanket on the floor, me trying to read while Erik tested the limits of his mobility. He had already started crawling, opening drawers, touching electrical outlets, you couldn't take your eyes off of him for a second. Goodbye, book. It's impossible to read like that. Have a little boob, let's see if it stops raining, eh?

I tortured myself with the idea of idyllic afternoons in a parallel universe: free to write, brimming with results. I imagined that the afternoons were necessarily more productive, under no circumstance would one suffer the same lack of inspiration typical of mornings, no way. In the afternoon—oh, the afternoon— words and sentences would spring forth naturally, the story would progress, inexorable, fresh, with rhythm, stirring. Later, at sunset, I would get in the car and take a ride to Durango, Agurain, Igorre, villages in which book clubs were waiting to welcome me sweetly, where I would talk about my novel—about myself, really—loving my words, loving my life. Once the gathering had come to an end, I would still have a time for a glass of wine and a *pintxo* with my readers—high school teachers, dynamic retirees, men with little pads of paper and lots of notes, cheerful, candid women—and I would resume my monologue, more informally now, and in passing mention some of my projects, the exotic research trip I had planned, and all the attendees would admire my talent, my youth, even my beauty. And when I'd reach for my wallet to pay for the drinks, they would put out their hands to stop me, what are you doing, stop that, it's our treat, an honor, please, come now, come on. And thus I'd return home, tired but content as only a writer can be after a productive day at work.

Instead of that scenario, I was changing diapers, doing load after load of laundry, taking out my tits every time the baby fussed, seeking increasingly sophisticated children's entertainment.

The thought of leaving Erik at daycare for longer buzzed in my brain like a fly. The temptation was strong, but I didn't know how I could justify it to either Niclas or Erik's teachers (they knew I didn't work, they had seen me spend hours in bars and cafes and, for some reason, I cared enormously what they thought of me). Above all, I didn't know how I could justify it to myself.

Every day when I picked him up, no matter what Erik was doing when I arrived, he would sense my presence and promptly abandon his activity. Then he would crawl to me, swift and happy, stretching out his little arms, his whole face lit up, *Mama! You came! Another day and I haven't been left here forever! I'm so grateful, you have no idea!* We would squeeze each other tight and I would tell myself I should wring everything I could from that moment, I should enjoy it, because I would never love a little body that same way ever again, the perfect spine, chubby cheeks, tender little bum, perfect skin just begging to be kissed. After all, that was life, too. Life in its purest state, unmarred energy, radiance. I was an idiot not to enjoy it the way it deserved. I had the sense that something was escaping me, something wasn't working right. If I could absorb that energy, that force, then surely it would show through in my writing: my intense contact with life would be present, one way or another, in my words.

Was that it?

I wasn't sure.

Summer was approaching and this opened up new opportunities. We'd agreed that we wouldn't take a vacation, we needed to be frugal and make the prize money go as far as it could. The only expected change in our routine was a visit from Niclas's parents for two weeks in August. But I had to see Léa. I had become convinced that in order to make any progress on my project, I would need to speak to my friend, one of the people who knew the young Jade best.

In our sporadic text exchanges, Léa continued to be as brief as ever about the subject. I'd had to explain to her, not uncomfortably, that I was writing about Jade's case. I told her that it was a newspaper assignment, something which had begun as a simple article but that, given the potential, was turning into a book. Coming up with this sort of harmless lie is very on brand for me. Absurd lies that don't change anything, and are undoubtedly directed at myself. (I can offer up one of my greatest hits as an example: once I had a cab ride that cost 8.76 euros; I gave the driver a ten, but asked him to give me a euro in change, then went on to improvise that I needed the euro to put under my daughter's pillow, because she had just lost her first tooth that very day. No such daughter existed, of course, I simply hadn't wanted to give him ten euros, but I also didn't want to seem cheap. In the end, the only thing I achieved was to feel ridiculous.) In the matter at hand, my lie was related to not wanting Léa to think I was macabre or an opportunist, to make her—and myself—believe that a deep, professional, and therefore acceptable, interest moved me to approach the topic.

My friend replied tersely to my messages, that was true, but I felt sure her attitude would change if we could meet face to face.

There would be the kind of total mutual understanding that leads to honest, illuminating conversations, the kind that change lives.

I found a solution. During the last days of spring, instead of writing, I used the daycare hours to look for deals on hotels, from the Costa Azul—too expensive—to the Costa Brava. I finally came across a hotel in Rosas three or four streets from the beachfront. Including half-board and everything, it turned out to be oddly inexpensive. The TripAdvisor reviews were mostly terrible—old mattresses, noisy at night, greasy buffet—but it fit our budget. And the hotel was family-friendly, which I thought was something I should take into account.

Admittedly, my financial situation was not the most stable: every extra expense robbed me of time to write, as it meant I would have to return earlier to work. On the other hand, the book was adamantly demanding the trip to see Léa.

I didn't explain my true intentions when I presented the plan to Niclas. I began by singing the praises of a week on the Mediterranean, especially for the baby, then went on to list some adult pleasures: paella, wine from the Empordà, the warm sea. I let drop the possibility of visiting Léa later, when the reservations had been booked, as if it had just suddenly occurred to me. It would be really good for my book. It was only a four-hour trip. One night away. Erik was about to be a year old and he had to start getting used to the breast not always being available. As in every negotiation, I had to throw in something, as well. I agreed that, come September, Niclas could get away for a night in the mountains.

It was easier than I had expected.

And so we set off the night before San Ignacio's Day, the three of us in the car. Little Erik did unexpectedly well on the drive, sleeping better in the car than at home. As we drove through Los Monegros desert in Aragón, I even allowed myself a little nap. A moment of peace, brought to us by air conditioning.

All the looming concerns about the hotel turned out to be valid. It was old and full of kids. The majority of guests were large families from Eastern Europe. While the parents wearing all-inclusive wristbands lounged on beach chairs, mojitos in hand, the hotel took charge of their offspring: water polo competition in the pool, archery and ping-pong tournament on the lawn, costume parties, crafts from various recycled materials, kitschy dance party at night. Occasionally, I spotted a childless couple or individual in the dining hall, chewing their toast alone, and I couldn't figure out how they'd been duped into staying at that hotel, and more importantly, why they hadn't already fled the tumult of wet flip-flops, athletic whooping, and sticky soft drinks.

Erik was too young to leave in the care of the two staff members wearing orange T-shirts who worked tirelessly from nine in the morning until nine at night, so we left the hotel in the morning and didn't return until it was time for dinner. The original plan involved spending the day at the beach, but we were promptly convinced of its impracticality after realizing that our extremely fair-skinned son was disgusted by the sand, frightened of the sea, and incapable of staying put under the sun umbrella or keeping a hat on his head. Furthermore, we were barred access to the prettiest, least crowded coves without a porter's assistance: toys, umbrella, cooler, sunscreens of all types, water bottles . . . getting around was a nightmare. We quickly decided to focus on cultural tourism. In the span of two days, we visited Cadaqués, Figueres, and Girona, always in search of shade.

We slept badly at night. The air conditioning didn't improve things, given that while it did cool the room, its deafening blast kept us from falling asleep.

On the fourth day of our vacation, after I'd pumped Erik full of milk, given him a few quick cuddles, and put on my saddest face, I started up the car and drove off alone. I don't think I've ever experienced a greater sense of freedom than the moment I got on the N-11, pushing the speed limit and following the signs for Perpinya-Peralada-La Jonquera.

I see Léa every two to three years, five times or so since our year together ended. We've made weekend plans in London and Paris, somewhat longer visits to our respective home cities. But the distance between us never grows; we have always greeted each other as if we'd been together the day before, we pick back up right where we left off. We share a common past—not a very broad one, but intense—and we know how to make use of it. Ours is a friendship that will never be sullied, a friendship treated with care, idealized by virtue of hardly seeing each other. We would be able to forgive each other anything.

Though they had recently moved to a town outside Avignon, we made a plan to meet in the city center at 8 P.M., in the plaza in front of the papal palace. I had to wait almost twenty minutes for her; the heat was still stifling, it was quite a bit worse than on the coast. My first beer didn't last long, and I didn't hesitate to order another. I didn't have to nurse Erik. I could get drunk for the first time in I couldn't remember how long.

Every year, I feel a celestial calling, an unmistakable sign of summer's arrival that changes my face and mood. Sometimes the sign came earlier than summer itself, with the first hot day in May, for instance. It might be something concrete—lying in the grass to stargaze, the distant echo of a block party, the first sip of a mojito with a lot of mint—or something more undefined, an ineffable feeling, the scent of an invisible ether, the suppressed excitement of everyone around you. That year, I got the sign in Avignon in front of the papal palace when I took the first sip of that second beer. It's summer. I'm summer. It was well into August by that point, but better late than never, I suppose.

It was my second stay in the French city. I had come seven years before, for the baptism of Léa's first son, and everything was more or less how I remembered it. I didn't see her two younger children—daughters, whose ages I calculated to be around two and four that summer—have to undergo the same ritual, which honestly didn't surprise me at all, considering the total disaster the first baptism and party to follow had been.

But I'll describe that later. Léa is just getting here. She's caught me well into my second beer, and we have a lot to talk about.

It was a Gascon, Bertrand de Got, better known as Clement V, who first established Avignon as a pontifical seat. Though it began as a provisional residence, during almost the whole of the fourteenth century, seven Popes found refuge in the palace, far from Rome and its plots and conspiracies. It's one of the largest Gothic structures in the world. According to the guides, its walls are five meters thick, but not impenetrable, as evidenced by my last visit to Avignon, when I managed to sneak into the palace through the gift shop exit when the security guard wasn't paying attention. I roamed its halls, expecting they'd catch me at any second. They never did.

But I'm not here for covert tourist activities now. Now, I need to hear from Léa. And here we are. A summer night. Floral dresses, sandals, our respective tattoos nicely on display (mine on my ankle, hers on her shoulder blade). Two beers on the table. And a lot to talk about.

To put it another way: we were young again.

So young that, in a burst of quasi-adolescent friendship, I'd been able to forget Jade/Alice. We talked about ourselves, and she was just herself and I was just me. Our conversation was peppered with memories from the past, plans for the future, trivial gossip, negligible mischievousness. I didn't have to check the time, I didn't have to nurse Erik. I didn't even have to think about not having to do it. But at some point, the pressure in my breasts became too much and I excused myself to go to the bathroom, where I literally milked myself into the basin of the sink. When I return to the table, there's no way we can avoid talking about babies.

Most of our old pals from AB have succumbed to the urge to procreate, but Léa was the pioneer. She was just twenty-three when Matthias was born. For many people, such a zest for reproduction is a byproduct of being in love; and while I believe this is true in Léa's case, her urgency to have a baby when we were young had always surprised me.

"Are you sure you want to stay in this hotel? You know we have plenty of room at the new house."

"Yeah, I'm sure. Please don't take it personally, but I'd like to spend a night on my own, even if it's only one."

"Okay, but don't think I'm going to let you turn in too early."

"I'm counting on it. Another beer? And let's order some food, I'm going to faint if I don't eat something."

She doesn't take it personally, and I'm sure she understands— even envies—me. Who better than Léa, with three little wild animals waiting for her at home.

I had booked a room in a familiar hotel, the small but charming Hôtel d'Angleterre, inside the city walls, where I had stayed seven years before. I came alone that time, as well; I had planned on being joined by my boyfriend at the time, a Colombian I'd met in London who had no problem telling me that he would rather chomp on light bulbs than join me in Avignon for a civil baptism (which he didn't even know the meaning of). We broke up soon after (which was predictable) and Niclas appeared in my life; as a result, the trip to Avignon and even the civil baptism had symbolized an important transition.

"The hotel is pretty nice," Léa told me on that first occasion. She had driven me over to check in, Matthias in the back in his car seat. "The best rooms look out over the boulevard."

There were numerous, legitimate reasons for having intimate knowledge of hotel rooms in your own city—floors being refinished at home, the need to break up your routine, etc.—but the way she said it gave me the impression that none of those reasons applied to her. I didn't press. I stepped out onto the balcony, which did not overlook the boulevard, but the parking lot around back.

"The hand soap is fantastic, from Marseille, mint," she added, and slipped into the bathroom to see if her information was still up to date.

My suspicions grew, of course, but instead of pressing her, I felt self-conscious and stayed focused on unpacking my suitcase. I'm naturally discreet, and embarrassment tends to get the best of me.

"Shit, my dress for the christening is a wrinkled mess," I said, honestly annoyed but relieved to find a reason to change the subject.

"Oh, dearie me!" she joked. "Whatever shall we do? I better make a few calls—we obviously have to call the whole thing off."

Ultimately, we were able to make the dress presentable by smoothing it out with our hands, and I showed up looking as decent as possible at the ceremony. The christening was held at the City Hall; the mayor wore a tricolor sash, there were speeches and possibly pompous words that I didn't understand. Civil baptisms originated in times of the Revolution in France, and I wasn't sure if, in the twenty-first century, the whole thing was meant to be taken ironically or seriously. In any case, Matthias was darling, blond, and loving with everybody; he spent the ceremony being passed from person to person, never losing his smile.

The dinner that followed was held at a hotel outside the city, next to a golf course. The garden was lovely, even boasting a pond. The food was very good, the place smelled of freshly cut grass, and the heat was beginning to be bearable. My Colombian boyfriend felt farther and farther away, very far, and thanks to the champagne, my understanding of French had dramatically improved and so I convinced myself that I wouldn't have much trouble meeting someone worthy of an invitation back to the Hôtel d'Angleterre: it was only a matter of playing my cards right.

It was almost midnight when Matthias's grandmother took the baby home. The adults remained at the hotel, sucking down cocktails their only responsibility.

I felt somewhat adrift, disoriented, but happy, too, and with my paltry linguistic resources tried to communicate and make others happy as well; I felt *sympa, très sympa*, even as I preyed on any waiter who happened to wander into my vicinity with one of those marvelous champagne-laden trays. But if I paused, if I paid attention, I could sense a strangely charged atmosphere. Léa's boyfriend, Albert, was drinking heavily, and every time Léa spoke to me it was to complain about the stupid party, all Albert's idea (of course!), and all the money they were spending on it. Initially, I chalked it up to the not-very-festive French national character.

Suddenly, then, Albert was on his knees, clinging to Léa's hips. The climax of the evening was upon us. At first blush it looked to be alcohol-induced declarations of love and devotion, but I quickly realized that the man was crying like a baby and Léa's face was full of disgust. Either the DJ hadn't caught on or he was a true professional (such hyper bizarre scenes must have been common in his line of work) because, in any case, the music played on and the majority of guests continued to dance as if nothing was happening. I, on the other hand, stood frozen, fixated on the scene. When Léa finally removed herself from Albert's clutches and fled the party, I went after her.

I found her in the bathroom, washing her face.

"Hey, I'll drive you back to your hotel. Shall we?" she said.

I accepted, not considering my would-be chauffeur's blood alcohol content. Thankfully we arrived in one piece, having ridden the whole way in silence. Léa parked the car and then told me she didn't feel like going home; the baby was spending the night at his grandmother's, anyway. I was happy to take her in, and on the bed in the Hôtel d'Angleterre, she filled me in on the whole story.

It was very simple, really. When she was three months pregnant, she met Fabrice, a dad at the school where Léa was doing her student teaching. It was an instantaneous bolt of lightning that sparked an unstoppable wildfire, no hackneyed metaphor could do better justice to explain what happened next. The thing simply got out of control and they couldn't stop it. They started seeing each other in the Hôtel d'Angleterre, four, five, six secret dates, as Léa's belly grew. The man (twelve years older, married, father of two) didn't mind. On the contrary, he seemed inclined to play father to that baby that wasn't his. This was how Léa spent her pregnancy, with child and caught up in a whirlwind affair with a married man. It was addictive, the thing between them, a cocktail of fear, guilt, and orgasms. There were many comings and goings, doubts, tears, cinematic gestures, final break ups that occurred every other week. I could imagine it perfectly: Léa was having doubts and Fabrice, who had his pride, agreed to back off; then came the harsh words, the rancor and spite; and after a few agonizing days, one of them would suggest they meet, for the last time, just to end on good terms, and they would see each other in the Hôtel d'Angleterre and the whole cycle would kick off again.

A month before she was due, Léa decided to end things for good. Quite suddenly she felt she needed to act sensibly. She was able to resist her lover during those final weeks of the pregnancy. But the night after the birth, she sent Fabrice a message from her hospital bed. Just to let him know everything had gone okay, she told herself.

It was during the baby's early days, while he was just getting habituated to life outside the womb, when Albert discovered the whole thing. And then came the real drama. Soon Fabrice's wife knew as well, and word reached the school where Léa did her student teaching. One could say that the entire population of the *département* of Vaucluse between the ages of eight and eighty knew the story.

I had to get up from the bed then, unable to stop the room

from spinning, and lose the little dignity I had left by vomiting noisily in the bathroom. When I rejoined my friend, she seemed calm, even sober. She picked up her story right where she'd left off. I curled into a ball and hid my head under a pillow.

"Taking a lover while pregnant with another man's baby—I broke a big taboo, didn't I? Maybe the biggest one of all."

Léa's story shocked me at the time. I was only twenty-four and my relationship history was as common as they come. How shocked we are by our friends' stories could be a good measure of our age and experience. Nowadays there are very few things that could leave me in the same state of shock as Léa's disclosure had. This unsettles me, it makes me feel like, by this point, we have emptied the glasses of our innocence.

Now, for instance, I wouldn't say that the biggest taboo is having a lover while pregnant.

Not by a long shot.

A brief aside, only because I'm concerned about making it clear that I am a cultured person. Chastity, in Roman times, meant safeguarding the caste. A woman expecting a baby could, in theory, go to bed with whomever she wanted, since at that moment the lineage was secure. This was how Julia, daughter of the emperor Augustus, answered when asked how she remained chaste: *Numquam enim nisi navi plena tollo vectorem.* In other words, I don't permit passengers aboard unless the wine cellar is full.

Chastity, in our times, isn't measured by how much lineage is protected, but rather by how much pleasure is suppressed.

They brought us a dozen oysters and two glasses of wine. I don't like oysters, actually, but I can never refuse when someone suggests them. I don't want to be a killjoy, even though I simply don't get their esthetic value. All my attempts at sophistication would fail if I were to admit that hey, to be honest, I don't like oysters. Besides, after such a prolonged period of abstinence, two cold beers (or had it been three?) had easily whisked me into that euphoric stage of drunkenness where I was capable of anything, even sticking that gluey, formless mollusk in my mouth. Why not? *Allons, enfants de la Patrie!*

It still felt out of place to bring up Jade. Summer, white wine, oysters, friends. Who wants to talk about a madwoman who killed her twins? Wasn't it better to forget that such things could even happen?

Fortunately, it was Léa who eventually brought up the reason for our getting together. And as we ate the oysters, she recalled how that madwoman had taught her to stick two fingers down her throat, and immediately thereafter gave me a fifteen-minute run-down of two childhoods, two adolescences.

They'd met soon after their sixth birthdays, and ever since they were always together. Jade was naughty, zany, full of mischief. She was brave. She also knew how to pretend that she was a good girl when the situation required it. More than once, Léa had had to pay the consequences for something Jade had done. She wasn't a good student, nor did she try to be. She didn't like to read and had no special talent for numbers. They took the bus to school. Jade always showed up at the bus stop alone, and alone she made her way back home when dropped off at the end of the day. She lived with her mother and a younger half-brother. She was often at Léa's house. Léa almost never set foot in Jade's. Jade's mother didn't work, she was half deaf and, since she had two kids, she received enough government help to survive. She was skin and bones, and smoked constantly. Maybe she drank, too. She always kept a bottle of Listerine next to the kitchen sink and would gargle right there, spitting onto the dirty plates. Léa found that absolutely disgusting. There was no father. Once, Jade told her that he was a handball player who fled Poland to live the capitalist dream, but that he had fled back around the time she was born. Her mother and the Pole had met in the hotel where the mother worked. She served him breakfast and he put a baby in her belly. Léa had no idea if there was any truth to all that. Jade herself wouldn't know, surely. Her face undoubtedly had something Slavic about it: her eyes, her sharp cheekbones.

(First oyster.)

After lunch in the school cafeteria, Jade took Léa by the hand and led her to the bathroom. There she showed her how to purge the food by sticking her middle and index fingers down her throat. It became their after-lunch routine. Models did it, too, it was a way of cleansing one's insides. The practice afforded Léa such satisfaction that she started doing it at night as well, at home after dinner. It didn't take her parents long to find out. They took her to a psychologist. They were eleven years old, and this was the first time they were kept apart. Jade wasn't a good influence, her parents said. It wasn't a good time. Better not to go into detail.

(Second oyster.)

They started *le collège*, and that gave them the opportunity to hang out again. That was when Jade started painting and earning praise from the teachers. Léa played the piano, but nobody bothered to encourage her much. From time to time—and keeping it a secret from her friend—she still threw up. Only sporadically, it wasn't cause for alarm. She didn't know if Jade still purged, as well, but Léa liked imagining that she did, that their retching brought them closer, united them on a level no one else could reach.

Jade opted for the fine arts track at high school, so she attended a different *lycée*. They would meet up in the city center, go shopping, do some minor shoplifting, waste hours down by the river, making plans, drinking gin. Jade always had a cohort of boys hanging around her, but she had no problem telling them to get lost so she could be with Léa. This filled Léa with pride.

Sometimes, she caught Jade in little lies, the importance of which she tried to minimize. Léa chalked it up to the shame she felt about her family, her ill-fated mother, her dumbbell of a brother. Her goal was now the School of Fine Arts in Paris, the best in the country. Delacroix, Monet, and Renoir had studied there, among others. The first requirement was to send a dossier of her work. Léa herself helped Jade select her best drawings and watercolors. She declared her honest admiration for those women's bodies that looked increasingly like snakes. They were both excited about the prospect of a Parisian adventure, although Léa had already agreed with her parents that she would study History at the University of Avignon.

Getting into the Paris art school was very difficult, but Jade was good. Her grades had improved notably during high school and her teachers were all crazy about her watercolors, those beautifully deformed women painted time and again.

One night in May, the phone at Léa's parents' house rang at eleven o'clock, startling the whole family. It was Jade. She had spent the whole day on cloud nine. A letter from Paris had arrived that morning. Her dossier had been accepted and they were summoning her for the in-person exam. She couldn't believe it. She was afraid she would wake from the dream at any moment. But Léa could believe it, she put all her faith in her friend. Nevertheless, as the date of the exam drew near, there was drama: Jade didn't have enough money for the trip. Her mother didn't want to chip in and, since it was May, the savings from her summer job—they had both worked a couple of summers at a souvenir shop—had long since been spent. Léa got her the money for the train and a hostel: a little from her own savings, a little from her mother's wallet.

Several days went by and Léa still had no news from her friend, though she was sure that Jade would do well. In her mind, it was an excellent plan: next year she would have someone to visit in Paris, someone, moreover, who would show her the city's most Bohemian corners and most interesting people. She saw it so clearly that when Jade told her yes, yes she had been accepted, Léa hadn't even been surprised. They went out to celebrate. The shots of tequila flowed, all on Léa's dime. When she got home drunk at four in the morning, she earned a memorable telling-off from her parents.

Halfway through the summer, more drama: after running the numbers, and based on the humble scholarship she was hoping to get, it turned out to be impossible to survive the school year in Paris. The city had become outrageously expensive: rent, bills, the shopping, art materials for the course . . . simply impossible.

And what if she got a little job in the evenings, the weekends? Léa asked. It wasn't recommended. The school was so strict, so demanding, and the competition so ruthless that outside of school hours one had to keep painting, practicing, studying.

(A longer pause, and the third and fourth oysters.)

They considered all possible solutions, the majority of which were zany schemes: putting an ad in the paper to attract a patron, getting in contact with her absent father (whom they imagined was undoubtedly the wealthy owner of an entire handball team by then) to ask for help, or finding a squatter-occupied building where Jade could live rent-free.

Of those options, the only really tempting one was the first. Léa paid by the word for a rather stupid announcement in the paper. No patron came out of it, but *La Provence* called Jade to participate with two other students in a long piece about the hardships facing students from the provinces who had to move to Paris. At the start of the twenty-first century, the world's largest metropolises were reinventing themselves and becoming more valuable, the elites started to take over, expelling the long-time residents, everyone's heard of the gentrification of London, New York, Paris. Within this context, Jade's words—not to mention her feline eyes—were a perfect fit for the newspaper.

(Fifth oyster and second-to-last sip.)

Unfortunately, a sponsor still hadn't appeared even after the article was published. Jade gave up. Too soon, according to Léa. Here was her big chance for change and she was going to let it pass all because of a few shitty francs. Moreover, it was too late to enroll in the University of Avignon: she would lose a whole year for the stupidest reason. But it was futile to talk to her, to try and convince her not to give up. Eventually even Léa came to accept it. They grew more distant after that. Léa started university and Jade started wandering the world. People said she was with some man, now in Toulouse, now in Marseille or Barcelona. She was no longer living with her mother, she came to the city sporadically, no one knew exactly how she made her money. Léa tried to be in touch as often as she could. She feared for her friend, anything could happen to her. Sometimes they spoke over the phone: everything was going great, she had modeling gigs all over the place, she was earning good money. Léa usually felt better after they talked. Maybe it was true that Jade was getting to know a wonderful new world, that she was finally happy. Meanwhile, what was Léa doing with her life? Living with her parents, wasting her youth on ridiculous classes. And Jade's painting? No, Jade wasn't interested in painting anymore, it was very lonely work; the social life was what she was really good at.

The opportunity to spend a year in England opened before Léa like a stage curtain parting. She could show her friend that she too had a calling for adventure. That's why she invited Jade to join her that first week. Léa would pay for her plane ticket, they would stay together in her room. It was an all or nothing proposal: the last chance to get back their lost closeness.

(Sixth and final oyster, and a burgeoning awareness of what has been ingested.)

"So how was it?" I asked as I drank the last drops of white wine, less out of thirst and more to rinse the mollusk-taste from my mouth.

"Well, what can I say, you were there: it was a disaster. Jade, until then, had been a woman of the world, and I was the snot-nosed little girl who had never left her parents' house. But as soon as she'd stepped on campus, the masks came off. She was out of her element, I don't know if you remember but she hid behind me like a little pup, scared, because she barely spoke English, that someone was going to talk to her. And that hurt her. That realization, or maybe the fear that I'd realized it. I think that's why she stopped speaking to me."

"You didn't have any more contact after she went back to France?"

"None. The earth swallowed her up. I called her, wrote I don't know how many emails. Soon after, I got a message back that her email address was no longer valid. I thought the worst. Later, I came to the conclusion that it was about escaping her lies, maybe to get herself set up in a new set of them. I suppose it was around that time that she changed her name."

"Which lies are you talking about?"

"Well, all of them. Do you really think there's any truth to what I've told you? Paris? Really? That art school accepts ten dossiers out of every hundred they get, and of those ten, only one is chosen for the in-person exam. I don't think Jade was that good, to be honest. She simply took my money, had a little holiday in Paris, and then made up that whole story about how the scholarship wouldn't cover her costs. I never did see any letter or official document from the school. I took her at her word. But now I doubt it all."

I wanted to ask about the name change, the possible connotations of Jade and Alice, but another question struck me first.

"When you were friends, did she ever talk to you about wanting to be a mother?"

"Never. She actually thought I was nuts when I told her I wanted to have kids young. And you know what? She was right about that. I was a complete idiot."

6.

FIRST BIRTHDAY

Having kids changes your life drastically, and I really love mine.
Children aren't the only things that bring you gratification and
happiness, and it's easier to give life than give love.

CAMERON DÍAZ, *InStyle*

Unstable, narcissistic, egocentric, charismatic, hateful, out of touch
with reality, frivolous, complex-ridden, suffering from low self-esteem, manipulative, selfish, false, aggressive, proud, dishonest, bad
actor, incomprehensible. All of that, for sure.

But capable of murdering two babies, her own tender, de-
fenseless children, brought into this world after such concerted
effort, in the coldest, most atrocious way? Absolutely not. Léa was
convinced. No one could have predicted such a thing. But really,
who could kill a child? No one. And since no one can, when a
child is murdered, we are all potentially suspect.

"No, impossible. No. And yet she did do it, didn't she? She
was capable of it. I can't think of anything to say, except maybe . . .
well, all I know is that pregnancy makes you crazy." Léa brooded.

We had moved to a different bar, one that didn't welcome
tourists, but sad, silent little men. It was one of the few bars still
open at that hour (ten-thirty!).

"What will happen to Jade now?"

"Who knows, could be anything. She could get off, or spend forty years in prison."

"When's the trial?"

"Sometime in the next few months. A date hasn't been set."

"Do you plan to go?"

"Maybe."

(Obviously, I planned to go.)

We drank in silence.

"You know, it was Fabrice, in my case. Totally the product of pregnancy and the 'fourth trimester.'"

"Really?" I didn't quite see the causal relationship.

"You have to remember that even back when you and I met, I was obsessed with having kids. I'd been fixated on the idea since I was sixteen. Then I got pregnant and was hit with all these doubts. Basic stuff that I'd ignored before. I started thinking about friends my age, about you, about how you'd stayed in England, enjoying London and your freedom. You were all enjoying the benefits of adulthood and none of the inconvenience. Not to mention Albert. I'd suddenly realized that I had chosen him for his qualities as a father and nothing else. I needed a release valve to feel alive, and fast. And Fabrice was there. That's the honest truth. If it hadn't been for Fabrice, I probably would have gone back to puking after meals. Or worse."

"Fabrice for you. Writing for me."

"And then when the girls were born, too." Léa ignored my interjection, immersed in a deep examination of her conscience. "I was desperate to be with him. I resisted when Laure was born, the melodrama was still so fresh and I wasn't interested in a repeat performance. But after Agnes, my youngest, I called him, I didn't care anymore. I knew there'd be no third chance if Albert found out, but I didn't care. Fabrice doesn't live here anymore, he moved to a little village in Provence, but he answered my call and we met up in a hotel outside the city. He and his wife had separated, but eventually they got back together. I'm sure he had a terrible time of it, too. I took the baby with me, she was just six weeks old. We had a glass of wine. We didn't end up in bed—he hadn't shown any interest. He looked sad to me, worn-out. He kept checking his watch and glancing around, he wanted to get out of there and well, a girl must have her pride. But if he'd been willing, I had it all worked out: when to give Agnes her bottle, how to get her to sleep, where to put the stroller, everything."

"Just as well, right?"

"I suppose it was for the best."

"Okay, but come on, there's a world of difference between that and Jade's situation."

"Of course there is. I guess what I'm trying to say is . . . Look, back before I became a mother, back when my idea of motherhood was so absurdly idealized, I would hear about women who abandoned their kids, or see it in a movie or something, and I'd find the story completely unbelievable. A mother would never abandon her greatest treasure. Nope, no way, a mother would sacrifice whatever was necessary and press on. I believed that shit. Did you ever see *Eyes Wide Shut*? It starts with Nicole Kidman confessing to her husband that she met a man at a hotel the previous summer, they'd just looked at each other, that was all, but in that instant she knew—without a shadow of a doubt—that she was capable of leaving everything if that man had asked her to, her husband, her daughter, her whole future."

"Yeah, I remember. Then the husband, Tom Cruise, goes crazy, wandering around the city—New York, right?—and joins in an orgy . . ."

"Yeah, ha ha. The poor guy is a mess, trying the whole night to rebuild his shattered masculinity. And why, in the end? Because he was forced to hear something that any woman, any mother, could be thinking any number of times throughout her life."

"It's true."

"See? You've realized it too—it's not like mothers possess some magical essence, nothing gives them an inherent ability to resist absolutely everything. And now I . . . look, I'm not saying it isn't horrible, obviously, but I do find them pretty believable now, those mothers who—under certain circumstances—abandon their children. Even the ones who end it all . . ."

I said nothing. I didn't want Léa to think I was agreeing with her just to be polite, but she was right: my own feelings had shifted in that same direction over the course of the past year. I thought of Sylvia Plath then, a figure I'd been nosing around for a while. Though I found her poetry somewhat hermetic, we happened to share the same birthday, October 27th, and I wondered if we might have some deeper connection that was worth chasing up.

Once, when I was living in London, I decided to walk to the house that had been Plath's last home, just north of Regent's Park, an hour and twenty minutes from where I worked. I chose a sunny afternoon in May. Of all the big cities in the world, London is probably the best for walking. Nobody would say so from looking at a map, the perspective of which makes it looks like a giant oyster with thousands of veins crisscrossing its body, a shapeless mass ready to swallow you up the moment you set foot on it. But on the surface, there are flowers, parks every two blocks, low buildings, elegant black cabs, doors painted in cheerful colors, cozy pubs. (Not totally true, anybody who arrives in London quickly learns that there are areas south of the Thames or to the east of the city that one should never set foot in, but those areas are erased, they cease to exist, and all that's left is walkable London, elegant and civilized under one's feet.)

It was eight o'clock in the evening, the time I usually got out of work (my life there wasn't nearly as free and easy as Léa had painted it), but the day wasn't over: May evenings are endless in

London, so I walked around enraptured by the scent of spring and its promises.

I knew I'd arrived when I spotted a blue plaque on the front of one of the buildings. The plaques are made and hung to acknowledge notable city residents. But it wasn't Plath who was memorialized at 23 Fitzroy Road; the distinction went to another poet: Irish, mystic, and father late in life, William Butler Yeats, who had also lived in that house as a child, about a hundred years before Plath. Since Yeats had lived there first, and been awarded a Nobel Prize, and had the good form not to commit suicide within those four walls, the plaque belonged to him. No sign of Sylvia.

Did I feel disappointment standing before that rather ordinary façade? White trim, blue building. Black wrought-iron fence with a little sign asking people not to chain their bikes up there. No. These sorts of pilgrimages are always internal, and I had found exactly what I was after. I spent a few moments imagining the beautiful Plath: on the other side of the wall, she prepared warm milk and toast for her children. She surely spread a thick layer of butter on the bread, as required by British custom. Then she would leave their breakfast on the children's night table, as they still slept. Then she would open the window and, having stuffed towels under the children's door, go down to the kitchen. She would close off the kitchen door, as well. All she had to do was turn on the gas, stick her head in the oven, and that's it. Goodbye, babies.

She was thirty. Her daughter Frieda, almost three. Nicholas, the baby, only three months old. I imagined Frieda the next morning, conscious of her role, offering her brother the milk, already cold. But apparently the people who found the body arrived before the children woke up.

Both births had been quick and easy for the poet, both at home (not that house, other places the family had lived), and described in abundant detail in frequent letters to her mother in the United States. The births of both babies had filled the poet's otherwise unhappy life with joy. There wasn't the slightest hint of anything like postpartum depression in her story. In the weeks after delivery, her creative drive came roaring back. Having arranged childcare shifts with her husband, Ted Hughes—otherwise the target of her feminist rage—Plath shut herself up in the study and wrote. It was in the period immediately following the birth of her second baby that she wrote *Ariel*, her best-known work. On March 4th, 1962, just six weeks after Nicholas was born, she wrote these lines, to her mother, which fill me with admiration and shame: *I am managing to get about two and a bit more hours in my study in the mornings and hope to make it four when I can face getting up at six, which I hope will be as soon as Nicholas stops waking for a night feeding.* In April she wrote: *I never dreamed it was possible to get such joy out of babies. I do think mine are special.* June 15th: *I don't know when I've been so happy or felt so well.*

Ecstasy in darkness.

But soon, once again and this time forever, only darkness.

I must have stood for five or six minutes in front of that house. I watched occupants come and go, I imagined the inside divided into apartments, compartmentalized in unexpected ways inside a dwelling that was once a single-family home. Before leaving, and still at risk of arousing suspicions, I spent a few more seconds on my vision of Plath's final minutes. Her goodbye kisses for the little ones she adored *every little bit of.* Her all-encompassing love for them made her suicide all the more unimaginable. If only for their sakes, wasn't it worth it to go on a little longer? Wasn't the simple prospect of watching Frieda and Nicholas grow up enough reason to stay alive? At least until the children were teens?

Apparently not.

Following Plath's suicide, her husband had another daughter with his lover, Assia Wevill. Although they lived together and Assia was a mother to the orphaned Frieda and Nicholas, they never married, and Ted Hughes never recognized his new daughter, a little girl as beautiful as her mother, whom they affectionately called Shura.

Life became hard. Assia was relentlessly harried by the ghost of Sylvia and, finally, in March 1969, she too turned on the gas. This time, there was something novel added to the family tradition Sylvia had started: Assia gave little Shura sleeping pills and settled her on a mattress in the kitchen; then, she turned on the gas and laid down beside the little girl. She held her daughter. Until it all went black.

Shura was four years old. Assia, the half-Jewish artist who, as a child, had managed to escape the Nazis, was forty-one.

In psychiatry, the term "extended suicide" is used in these cases. Sylvia Plath's son Nicholas Hughes also killed himself, in Alaska in 2009. That's how far the blond poet's suicide extended, the macabre family tradition. All the way to Alaska.

Uluru.

Dingo.

Rhodesia.

Alaska.

"If she'd at least committed suicide . . ." Léa says suddenly, confirming my suspicions that she can read my mind.

"We'd even have compassion for her, without spending two seconds on the kids."

"Exactly."

"But she didn't kill herself, fuck, she's still alive, she lives with what she did. That's the worst part."

"The worst."

We stared at the bottle of wine between us. Neither of us had anything else to add.

I wanted to know more and, at the same time, wanted to remain ignorant. I started to have the impression that the more Léa talked about Jade/Alice, the more the mystery unraveled. And I couldn't do anything with the scraps. The picture of the woman was quite clear, Léa was perceptive and knew how to get to the bottom of things, but what if at that bottom there was nothing at all? Erratic teenager, brought up in an unstructured family environment, suffering from one or more undiagnosed mental illnesses? It wasn't a very original tableau—even clichéd, one could almost say. A well-defined portrait that didn't help explain the acts.

It was appropriate, then, to distance oneself from reality. Move closer to fiction. And trust that, through one of the cracks, something true would escape.

Or maybe we simply needed to change bars again and keep drinking. The bad thing was that we were in Avignon, it was late, and our only option was to head to a dance club. Léa suggested a stroll along the Rhône, have a look at the broken bridge all lit up. I happily accepted. She used to hang around there as a student, with a book under her arm, and for a moment she was overcome by nostalgia: since they had moved out of the city, she almost never visited the center, she was almost forgetting the walls, the murmur of the river, the bridge.

"How do you imagine it?" We'd been walking in silence for several minutes. "What kind of state was she in, there beside the bathtub? Rage? Alienation? Indifference?"

"I've thought a lot about that." My friend took almost a minute to respond. "And honestly, I don't know which hypothesis is more terrifying. I can understand rage, that uncontrollable moment when everything just explodes. Would they not stop crying? Did she feel incapable of calming them? Did she lose it? An irrational impulse and an act that cannot be undone. It could have been like that. But, what if she did it calmly, decisively? Undress the babies, put the first one in the bath, gently press its head under the water. And when the little thing starts waving its arms and legs, wanting to cling to life, eyes wide open, looking at its own mother . . . keep going. When its face turns blue . . . keep going. Keep going until it's over."

"And then repeat the process with the other baby."

"Who was first? The boy, surely."

"I think it was the girl."

I don't know why I said that. It was so flippant that I appalled myself. I felt a curdling in my stomach that rose to my throat. I got as far away from Léa as I could and threw up at the edge of the water. My malaise floated off in the direction of the Mediterranean.

"Wow, this is your classic move in Avignon," said an amused Léa.

"It was the oysters. I knew it," I joked back.

But the truth was, I was crying. I stood off to the side a few moments longer, protected by the darkness, sick to death of it all.

There are some things that can't be talked about, and that was precisely why I had to write about them. Even if it wasn't right.

Back at the hotel, in a room that might well have been the scene of one of Léa's rendezvous, I took out my notebooks and attempted to write down on paper everything the night had supplied. When I'd finished, I returned to the bathroom to squeeze the milk from my breasts, but only a few drops came out: the body quickly adapts. It was three o'clock in the morning when I finally turned out the light and descended into a sticky, restless sleep that lasted six hours, six hours I spent strangely alone.

My stomach was still unsettled in the morning. I skipped breakfast and got right on the highway. Before crossing the border, I stopped at a rest area where I wolfed down a giant chocolate macaron and an equally giant coffee, then poked around the store a bit. I picked up a small wooden train, a classic, which turned out to be stupidly expensive. It seemed an appropriate present for the little Viking who was waiting for me at the family resort and who, the very next day, would celebrate his first birthday.

In the days and weeks that would follow—and for the first time since the day I delivered Erik—my thoughts were far removed from Jade's story. My notebook stayed closed and I hardly thought about my visit with Léa. It made me feel sick, and I was left with as little desire to eat oysters again as reread the lines I'd previously written. I had thought that being with Léa and getting her firsthand, real-life impressions of Jade would be the boost I needed. I couldn't have been more mistaken, because as much as I'd enjoyed the time with Léa and the night I'd spent on my own, the Avignon getaway had produced the exact opposite effect.

The rest of our vacation was fine. Nobody had been traumatized by my twenty-four-hour absence. We wound up adjusting to the schedule imposed on us by the hotel. Eventually, Erik overcame his fear of water and we were able to organize a little party for him beside the pool, where we invited a ton of kids to have cake with us. Soon after we returned home, Niclas's parents arrived and our hosting responsibilities took up all of our time: my in-laws showed up in Biscay eager to summit every mountain in the province. I was exhausted by the time they left, but my fatigue was purely physical: my head felt light and easy, nothing troubled me much, there were no hints of clouds on the horizon. I really enjoyed Erik during those August days. He had just started walking, coming at me with outstretched arms, squealing with joy and disbelief over his own amazing feat. When he reached me, I felt my heart ready to explode with equal parts love and pride, and I thought: they blossom so fast, right before our eyes, and we're so busy raising them we hardly notice.

The days passed, September drew near, and I was still powerless in summoning the urge to write. What if the drive simply never returned? What if I never finished the book? If I did, would anybody actually want to read it? What if I was doing humanity a favor by not writing it, allowing the incident to be lost in the sewer of history? Would it matter, I wondered, if I never wrote anything ever again?

But the fact remained: I'd taken leave, a decision that had impacted our family life, and now I couldn't just stick what I'd written in a drawer and say, ah well, I'll leave it as is. Nor was I certain about giving up on writing forever, either. Who would I be, if that part of my identity was castrated, silenced? What would I become? From the most mundane point of view, wouldn't a decision like that prove my staunchest critics right?

There was also a middle solution: adapt the project. After all, no one knew specifically what I was writing about. Jade's case could discreetly fall away; I could hang on to research I'd done, plus my own experience with motherhood, and create a kind of essay-diary-chronicle. But was there anything interesting to tell beyond percentiles, teeth, tears, constipation, and diarrhea? I immediately set to imagining the result: a mix of affection and complaint, exhaustion and love, disappointment and infinite tenderness, page after page, over and over, an ambivalent, tiresome mess that would make anybody queasy. A nightmare.

I thought that what I needed was to go back to work. My job has elements of creativity—as much creativity as designing marketing and communication plans for dental clinics demands— and the routine of work, with its miseries and achievements, would give me much needed distance and perspective. I prepared myself to put the manuscript on ice until then. *Sine die*. The impetus to finish the book would come. If it was meant to.

On the last day of August, which was also our last day of summer vacation, we spent the afternoon at a sidewalk bar, drinking beer mixed with soda water while Erik played at our feet, collecting olive pits and used paper napkins. Apathetically, I flipped open a newspaper and found myself faced with a piece of information that was destined to mess up my plans: according to the grease-stained page, Alice Espanet's trial was imminent. Jury selection was planned for mid-September, after which everything would be set into motion. The news was like a slap to the face; it caught me completely off guard. I had been counting on more delay. Another six months, a year. But no: fourteen months after the alleged crime, they were ready to go to trial, a sure sign the investigation had gone smoothly.

A sense of knowing spread through me again, only of an opposite ilk: I *had* to be present in that courtroom, unruffled, tuned in, intent on every word, every gesture. I needed to see Jade/Alice's face, hear her voice, scrutinize her eyes. I could not miss this opportunity, and the signs were clear. The news had come early and unexpectedly, just in time to catch me as my ambition faltered. In the trial lay the crucial elements I needed to finish my book. I saw it so clearly, it was all so natural, that I wasn't the least surprised to revert, then and there at the bar, to the same state of obsession that had consumed me a year earlier.

I was glad to have it back.

The only problem I could see was a logistical one. The very next day, briefings on my desk and office coffee would be waiting for me: I had only a few hours to make arrangements—at work and home—to extend my leave.

The state of my bank account, at the end of the summer and after an unexpected dental implant for Niclas: 4,407 euros.

PART II

VIOLENCE

1.

KILLING CHILDREN

It's a hard world for little things.

LILLIAN GISH, *The Night of the Hunter*

Ladies and gentlemen of the jury, first of all, take a breath, exhale, relax your jaw. The best thing you can do is stop being so scandalized. Maybe what you need now is a little historical perspective. Because this, as you'll understand, is nothing new. On the contrary, we can say that it is as old as humanity itself: people have always done away with children, babies, newborns. Why? The reasons are varied, but—observe—it essentially comes down to one thing: it's easy to kill a child. They're small, weak, incapable of organizing, demanding their rights, rising up, sharpening the guillotine, returning the blow. This is the truth and I'll say it again: killing children is easy. Quite a bit easier than killing full-grown, strong, powerful men. So easy that (think about it!) you don't have to do anything at all. If abortion demands *action* (be it turpentine or a rusty, unsterilized hanger to the uterus), infanticide only requires *omission*. Don't keep it warm, don't feed it or care for it, abandon it in a forest, lock it in a closet, forget you put it there. Done.

And not only that, ladies and gentlemen. Historically speaking, killing children, your own children, hasn't even been considered a crime. Why? Well, because, like women and slaves, children have always been considered property, property of their parents, as it were. Even today this is still the case, to some degree.

In fact, over the centuries, infanticide has been the most effective way to control the birthrate (reliable contraception being a recent invention). Is it not logical, if one considers it coldly? Until well into the twentieth-century, abortion was a high-risk practice for the mother (and still is in most parts of the world); but abandoning the newborn in the woods, by contrast, did her no harm. In ancient Rome, if a family wanted to adopt a baby, they knew they could go to the dumping grounds: there were always newborns there, and with a bit of luck, they might find one that was still alive.

The practice of eugenics represents another principal motivation behind infanticide throughout the centuries. Greek physician Soranus of Ephesus, now considered the father of gynecology, wrote a short guide on how to pick out children who were worth raising from those who were not. Throw it in the river, was his advice if the infant didn't meet certain criteria. Raising a child demands serious energy and resources: best to be sure it will be a good investment. More children will come. Healthier and stronger. More children always come. They're stubborn like that. In Sparta, this practice was taken to the extreme. The State itself took charge of selecting those apt for survival after an inspection of all newborns: there were those destined to be soldiers, and those who were immediately disposable.

Thousands of years later (history also has its wormholes), similar practices were carried out in Nazi Germany with the desire of optimizing the Aryan race. As soon as they were born, the premature, the deformed, and those suspected of being retarded were transferred to wards called *Kinderfachabteilungen*; there, a small dose of phenobarbital courtesy of Bayer Laboratories was enough to erase those defective little Germans from history. The Reich's pediatricians, midwives, and nurses were obliged to participate in the extermination by reporting the births of "special" children in exchange for some small financial compensation. And just look, they did such an excellent job that in only a few years, they caused a genocide of more than ten thousand babies. Meanwhile, abortion was illegal in Germany and any woman who had one, or even tried, got the death penalty.

But let's stick to a teleological evolution of history, ladies and gentlemen; I wouldn't want to dizzy you with too much skipping around.

In Rome, infanticide was not merely a common practice but one protected by law, at least until Christianity's arrival. The primitive Laws of the Twelve Tables: it was within the power of the *pater familias* to free himself of offspring born with a defect. Until the fourth century, infanticide was common currency if the parents couldn't or didn't want to provide for the newborn, or if it unfortunately happened to be a girl. *If it's a girl, get rid of it*, one wealthy merchant wrote to his pregnant wife. (Fortunately, only China and India still cling to the custom of ridding themselves of female young. Unfortunately, nearly half the world's population lives in those countries.)

The murder of children is also a way men have attempted to please the gods. In Mayan jungles and powerful Carthage, on Celtic lands and frozen Siberia, infanticide took shape as divine offering. Though it was just a macabre joke in the end, Abraham of the Old Testament didn't find God's request to kill his son Isaac particularly strange or scandalous. In fact, he built an altar, readied the wood, and bound Isaac, who was shaking like a lamb to the slaughter.

And the most powerful kings, too, have plotted infant holocaust as if they were designing geopolitical strategy. Some ordered the massacre of all children under the age of two, without taking into account the ruinous demographic consequences: the pharaoh in the time of Moses and the copycat Herod of Judea. Poor innocents.

But breathe, ladies and gentlemen. History marches on and these practices fall behind; contrary to popular belief, the past is *always always always* much worse. At least until now. Constantine, the first Christian Roman Emperor, rejected the practice of infanticide and it was after his death that a revolutionary idea began to take hold: *infanticide as a type of homicide*. What?! But they're just kids! Well, sure, but even so.

Regardless, the role of the Catholic Church is paradoxical in this respect: on one hand, it fights the scourge of infanticide, and on the other it condemns—with inexhaustible vigor—every child born out of wedlock to endless misery. Indeed, until well into the eighteenth century, bastard children enjoyed no rights: protected by no laws they were fugitives, pariahs, outcasts forever condemned to bear the sins inherited from the mother.

And what about that other religion? Well, chapter 17:31 of the Koran explicitly forbids infanticide: *Do not kill your children for fear of want. We will provide for them and for you. Surely killing them is a great sin.*

Here we have another compelling reason. A child, a mouth. In other words: another child, another mouth . . . among too many hungry mouths. God, we are told, will provide. But can this supply be guaranteed?

It was Thomas Malthus, an Anglican cleric, who first warned about the potential for human population growth compared to the much more limited ability to produce the means for subsistence. The predictable consequence was the Malthusian catastrophe, a disaster of biblical proportions that could only be attributed to little boys' and girls' stubborn insistence on being born. You only have to read between Malthus's lines to infer that since the instinct to reproduce is unstoppable, the desirable thing would then be to control all those new mouths coming into the world, preferably by closing them forever. But in that case, how do we square the divine command to be fruitful and multiply?

A few decades before, in 1729, another Anglican cleric by the name of Jonathan Swift found a compromise: he recommended that his poor Irish compatriots sell their children—preferably those under a year of age—as foodstuffs. The rich, he claimed, would know how to appreciate the child as a delicacy, and the little ones would go to a better place as a fricassee or ragout, which was a more decent fate than the death by starvation that awaited them. It was a practical solution for the poor of Ireland and a small luxury for rich gourmets: a win-win situation, as we say today.

I see the disapproval on your faces. Very well, it's not the time for satire. After all, reality has given us cases where mothers, in effect, ate their children out of pure desperation, and not that long ago: in Ukraine for example, during the great famine under Stalin. Okay, okay. I won't go into it.

But I would like to leave you with this idea: we progress, sensibilities become more refined, humanism spreads. At a certain point, the law stops making exceptions for infanticide, even in the case of illegitimate children. Killing them is bad and carries legal consequence.

This doesn't mean that it stops. It simply means that, under threat of harsh punishment, it starts to be performed in secret.

And thus, step by step we move ever closer to the case concerning us today. Once an almost systemic practice, infanticide becomes the extreme act of desperate mothers. From the Middle Ages to the nineteenth century, the most oft-wielded reason for killing a newborn is honor. From Goethe's *Faust*, we find an excellent example in the figure of Gretchen, a literary archetype born at the end of the eighteenth century. The story goes that Faust obtains sexual favors from Gretchen thanks to a pact with the Devil. Gretchen bears a child in consequence and in an attempt to conceal her dishonor, drowns the newborn without a second thought. The woman is sentenced to death for her crime. Faust cannot allow it—he is in love, after all—and turns to the Devil once more, this time for help securing the release of his seduced (raped?) lover. But it's too late for the girl: unable to face what she has done, she loses her mind; she has no desire to escape and, consumed by guilt, dies in Faust's arms. Another lost soul. Another eternal punishment.

We find another iteration of the same story in Catalan literature: Víctor Català (real name: Caterina Albert) penned the monologue *La infanticida*, first prize winner of the Jocs Florals d'Olot in 1898. The plot, in short: seduction, sex, pregnancy, sudden disappearance of the man, devastating arrival of the baby, desperation, grindstone, milling of tiny bones, authorities, madhouse for life.

If we leave the realm of Romantic literature and jump to raw reality, we can look at what was happening in Victorian London, if I still have your attention, ladies and gentlemen. In that prosperous metropolis, which was Hell for the proletariat, housemaids were well-aware that they stood to lose their position if they resisted "seduction" by the gentlemen of the house. Unfortunately, if the maid fell pregnant as a result, she was summarily dismissed. (This isn't entirely true: we have to look no further than Karl Marx, who convinced his maid to give their child up for adoption; there have always been good men.) Let us dedicate ten seconds to the predicament faced by those maids: out on the street, isolated, bereft of resources, her dishonor increasingly visible, and all consequence of a "seduction" she couldn't refuse. Under these circumstances, it's not hard to imagine her newborn's fate.

Queen Victoria herself had to intervene so that, in the case of infanticide, all of those fallen women wouldn't receive the death penalty. And so begins once again the history of infanticide as legal exception. Because an instance of infanticide can't be the same as homicide; not if committed by the mother, at least. This point of view is still reflected in current penal codes. In Spain's case, from 1822 to 1995 infanticide was considered a different crime than homicide. "The mother who, in order to conceal her dishonor, kills her newborn shall receive the minimum prison sentence; maternal grandparents who commit said crime in order to conceal the mother's dishonor shall receive the same sentence," read the law. Posterior draft amendments foresaw the dishonor motive's replacement with another element, that of the emotional strain produced by the circumstances of delivery and the postpartum period. The punishment: six months to six years. With the new Criminal Code of 1995, the crime of infanticide disappears completely. A mother who kills her baby in Spain today may perfectly well be sentenced for murder.

This isn't the case everywhere. Take Canada, for example. In that commendable North American country, if a mother kills her child under the age of a year as the result of an altered state owed to pregnancy, childbirth, or lactation (really? lactation?), she is committing infanticide. And this crime is exempt from punishment. All that is required is evidence of a mental disorder, anything to certify that pregnancy, childbirth, or lactation have left her completely loony. And what is usually brandished as proof? That she killed her kid! What else do you want? With this perfect tautology, the infanticidal mother avoids jail in Canada. It's a law currently under debate, critics claim it's a holdover from the Victorian age. But it remains in effect. And is worth keeping in mind.

Let us focus, ladies and gentlemen. The task before you is an extraordinary one. Therefore, it's in your interest to be clear on things. Children have always been murdered. Even nowadays. We're just more horrified by it. We are very horrified, indeed. In our collective imagination, the pedophile, the kidnapper in the park, the depraved child murderer is the monster par excellence. Still, the massacre of innocents continues. In the summer of 2014, the Israeli army assassinated four hundred children in Gaza, that cursed territory that's only forty kilometers long. A child under five is killed every other day in Mexico City. Estimates point to child deaths accounting for 27 percent of casualties in attacks carried out in Syria. Numbers of children dead are always cited in order to illustrate the horrors of war. But that doesn't stop the carnage. Or the wars. An image of a drowned three-year-old brought the plight of refugees to the front page. But this opened Europe's doors but a crack, which were swiftly closed.

Okay, I understand, you haven't come here to think about wars and bombings. Nor is it necessary. Outside the context of war, the danger to children resides in our homes in our peaceful, civilized West. In Europe, domestic violence kills thirty-five hundred children each year. Although Euripides gave us the story of the woman who kills her kids to hurt the husband who abandoned her, we can say unequivocally that the modern-day Medea is a man. Over the last decade in Spain, fifty-some-odd divorcing men have done away with their children in hopes of destroying the mother. Not for nothing, but modern interpretations of Medea focus on the conflict between her masculine and feminine sides: the masculine side calls for action, terrible but heroic, the sacrifice of her children for a greater cause. But the feminine side, caregiving and maternal, resists and pleads for the children's lives to be spared. Euripides portrays how the masculine position is the one that wins.

Norma, the Gallic high priestess in Vincenzo Bellini's opera of the same name, backs down after advancing on her children with knife in hand. Betrayed by Pollione, her lover and the children's father, Norma sees no other way out. Yet the feminine side finally prevails and she lets the little ones live.

You might tell me, and rightly so, that strictly feminine mothers kill their children as well. Indeed, if that weren't true then what would you, ladies and gentlemen of the jury, be doing on this bench, in this solemn chamber, charged with this tremendous responsibility?

It's not something openly discussed, but the truth is that post-partum mothers are always slipped the following piece of advice: *if you have suicidal thoughts or the urge to hurt the baby, get help.* The midwife is the one who keeps an eye on the woman who has just given birth. The health services pamphlet that all postnatal mothers are given also mentions these thoughts, these urges. A week after delivery, at the routine check-up, the midwife will ask: "How's your mood? Any dark thoughts?" And she'll give the baby a once-over, looking for warning signs. There is a reason for this.

Esteemed members of the jury, honorable ladies and gentle-men: eugenics, revenge, excessive Malthusianism, seduction, dishonor, poverty, utter destitution, unwed mothers, bastard children and hereditary sin, emotional strain of the postpartum period, extended suicide, postpartum depression, lactation-induced madness, mania unbound, mothers undone.

I know.

We cannot understand it.

You cannot understand it, can you?

They challenge our preconceived notions, these mothers.

This mother, specifically.

It's no small task you've been charged with.

I'm going to be here, crouched in the audience. I wouldn't want to be in your skin. This is my place.

2.

JADE/ALICE

One often hears that women "have bellyaches"; true
indeed, a hostile element is locked inside them: the
species is eating away at them.

SIMONE DE BEAUVOIR, *The Second Sex*

Nobody would deny Alice's beauty. It's like a hook: she casts and you take the bait. She has that aura that radiates off her, wherever she goes. The ideal proportions between throat and forehead. The perfect angle of spine and shoulders. She moves lightly through space. And so, everything is easier, everywhere (the crib, the bed, the bar, the office, the grocery store line), with the possible exception of the defendant's bench.

Nonetheless, up to now, her beauty has been nothing but an asset. Not for nothing, but panda bears owe their survival to being so cute. They eat a diet exclusively of bamboo. With a twelve-year life expectancy, they don't begin to reproduce until the age of seven, and the female is only fertile five days a year. If she happens to have two cubs, the mother will only concentrate on one of them, condemning the other to death. Pandas should have been extinct long ago, according to Darwin. But since they remind us of our stuffed animals from childhood, we protect them with loving care. That's the only reason they're still with us.

Alice, are you a panda, too? Of course you are, a warm, soft panda who birthed two babies and had to kill them both. What a pretty panda. At first glance, anyway.

But then come the misgivings, the need to peek behind the Wizard's curtain. Because beauty, until proven otherwise, feels suspicious in the long run. The myth of the femme fatale has added mortal danger to female beauty. *La belle dame sans merci*, as the Romantics would say. Alice's chestnut hair is shiny, of medium length, wavy. In the right dress, she would be perfect for a Pre-Raphaelite portrait. Pale face, red lips, enigmatic expression.

Beautiful and merciless, no doubt about it.

She's wearing light eye makeup today. Her outfit is subdued, as is usual in these cases: black pencil skirt, white blouse with a large bow at the neck, flats. Everything measured, planned, agreed upon with Carmela Basaguren, her lawyer. They did a test run and decided that her face looked too stark with her hair pulled back. Hands on the table at all times, resting before a blank piece of paper and black pen. She doesn't touch them. She has nothing to hide. Carmela Basaguren whispers something to her. Alice nods. She keeps her eyes straight ahead. I'm on tenterhooks.

Here we are again, at last, you and me. I see you. Will you see me? Will you remember me?

I hope not. Alice, Jade, where have you been since the last time I saw you, in a dorm on a small campus in the west of England? How did you wind up here, on trial in Vitoria, with me agog in the sixth row? What does your future hold, if you still have one, that is? Do you think about the future, or have you accepted defeat: no more todays, no more tomorrows, no compass, calendar, clock?

The judge arrives in his robe. To his right, the members of the jury. They look more sad than solemn. They have to decide what to do with you. On the judge's left, forming a perfect U, the prosecutors, the attorneys, you.

What to do with you, Alice? What to do with you, Jade?

Humanity has been imaginative with its criminals; the answers to the questions above plentiful and diverse: hard labor in a quarry, galleys, trenches, *via crucis*, walks of shame, dismemberment by horse, Brazen Bull, head on a pike, public stoning, breasts lopped off, Siberia, Guyana, Australia, poison hemlock, the fire, the sword, the gallows, the cliff, the garotte, the guillotine, the electric chair, lethal injection.

No, Jade; easy, Alice. There'll be none of that for you, rest assured.

The justice system has advanced. Here, now, it isn't the body that's punished, but the soul. Not the crime that's judged, but the ghost.

And yet, Alice does have a body, and that body may see forty years of jail time. Forty years of frisking and showers and line ups and head counts. Forty years of yard time, eleven steps forward and eleven back, everything measured, letters opened, aluminum trays, lights that go on and off according to somebody else's schedule. Walls, fences, boundaries. The body is in there. Who knows about the soul. The ghost.

That ghost of Alice's, which evades capture and leaps from one member of the jury to the next, slipping undetected in and among the judge's papers, now sliding down the prosecutor's robe. The body waits. Concrete, solid at this exact spot in sidereal space. In front of us all. This body, which is not just any body. White clay, fired in a good kiln. How much influence on this trial can a body like hers have? I see her profile; the jury has her right in front of them, hour after hour, day after day. Her cat eyes. The dance of her eyelashes. Her neck. Her shoulders. Her proportions. The black skirt and white blouse. A panda. She does not hide.

I've seen Ritxi, too, though I'd almost forgotten his existence, absorbed as I've been in the black hole that is Alice. He is sitting in the front row with two other men and a woman his age. His bald spot hadn't been noticeable in earlier pictures I had seen of him. Or maybe the hair loss is the result of this dramatic last year. He barely moves, he's a statue; but when he turns slightly to speak to his companions, I'm sure it's him: wine entrepreneur, Led Zeppelin fan, childless father.

Silence reigns, the first tense moments. It's the first day of class, maybe from here on out moods and manners will relax, but for the time being, I also try not to move, not to make noise, not to study Alice too openly. What would happen if she were to look back toward the sixth row and recognized my face? Would she comb her memory and locate me in another point in time and space, far away from here, an earlier age? What would she think? That I'm a ghost from her past, brought here in a prosecutorial ploy to remind her that she was once Jade, to break her once and for all? But she doesn't look, and if she did at some point, she wouldn't give me half a second of her attention; she has more important things on her mind.

Everything is aseptic and follows a clear-cut procedure. The judge—a perfectly ordinary man in his fifties—gives instructions, mostly to the jury. He seems bored. The cynicism of a man who has seen it all. Or maybe it's just a strategy to demonstrate impartiality, refined through years of experience on the stage. Five women and four men between the ages of twenty-five and sixty make up the jury. Some take notes, just for something to do. They're scared, but somewhat excited as well. They'll have something to talk about at home, which is always something to be grateful for.

So far, no one has mentioned the children. It is *the acts* that are referred to again and again.

Then the judge calls Alice Espanet to the stand. I didn't expect it to be so soon. Just like the news of the trial itself, this bit also catches me off guard. The first serious ripple runs through the audience when Alice states her name before the microphone.

Her voice, pronunciation, delivery, rhetoric; her body language and clothing and canny distribution of dramatic effects, the balance between reason and emotion, judicious use of metaphor, prudent, clear-cut, definitive conclusions. All of it matters in this piece of theater, as in any piece of theater. What is my first impression? That she's nailed it. She speaks perfect Spanish, though her accent is very strong. She pauses to find the precise word. She hasn't lost her nerve, not even under questioning by the female prosecutor, who—by the way—happens to resemble a parrot: big nose instead of a beak and dyed mahogany hair for ostentatious plumage; her voice is admittedly unpleasant, always forced, a good three pitches higher than what would be natural. By comparison, Alice modulates her voice, directs it where she wants it to go, she has absolute control over her vocal cords.

Her worst nightmare, says Alice, the now childless mother, when they ask her to describe the events in her own words. The call of the phantom. A call she heard from the beginning and tried to ignore. It was the reason she hadn't wanted to be alone with the babies, because she knew that one day she would no longer be able to resist, she would have an especially weak day and get carried away. And yet around the time the events occurred, she had been feeling better, or thought she was. Painting had helped. And she had started spending time alone with the babies. Just a few hours, the quietest ones. And that was when the shadow of the phantom loomed over her. At the moment she least expected it. She doesn't remember the details. Suddenly, everything went dark. And when a draught of air finally cleared away the black clouds, she saw her children on the bed, wet, cold. She tried to nurse them, both of them, though she'd never done it before. She saw it was impossible. She doesn't remember anything else until waking up in the hospital.

And that's when, for me, the spell is finally broken. There is nothing but a little gray man behind the curtain, desperately pulling strings. What's the point of this confused litany of cheap clichés, Alice? Nightmare? Phantom? Clouds? Amnesia? Jade, I expected better. I expected to believe you, understand you, even. A detailed, logical account.

Why do we look for esthetic value in murder, in the murderer? Isn't the criminal always a pathetic creature, miserable, worthy of pity? Why so many novels, films, TV shows? What is the point of all the effort to make sophisticated what is just evil ordinariness? Why do they make us swallow so many oysters? This here is a killer. Look at her, she is amorphous, viscous. She is pitiable and disgusting.

But I must be the only one looking at this broken mirror. Two members of the jury discreetly wipe their tears. The entire courtroom is stunned. When the questioning is over, the judge dismisses Alice to her seat. She rises, smooths the pencil skirt that has inched up her thighs, and returns to her lawyer's side. Calmly, eyes on the floor. Carmela Basaguren touches her briefly, affectionately, on the shoulder. The judge calls for a fifteen-minute recess.

It became my routine. The bureaucratic proceedings, the legal jargon, the black robes . . . it all helped me see things from a distance, with the same professionalism as the law students watching from the gallery. I arrived punctually, took my seat in the sixth row, tried to avoid the journalists—occasionally, I spotted a familiar face among the photographers—and waited in line at the coffee machine without striking up a conversation with anybody. I took lots of notes; by day four of the trial, I had already filled half of the black notebook I'd bought for the purpose. I was spending a small fortune on gas, tolls, blue zone parking. The sessions usually went until two or two thirty. If they finished at two, I still had time to eat a slice of potato omelet at the bar closest to the court building before driving back to Bilbao. I frequently found

Carmela Basaguren there, as calm as could be, having a glass of white wine. If the session went a little later, I didn't have time for lunch and had to make the trip with a belly full of coffee from the machine, feeling faint.

I was beginning to understand that trials are nothing more than a battle over narrative. Fundamentally, two opposing stories face off. Two narrative artifacts that, although different, are actually composed of the same elements—mythemes—arranged in different ways. Don't hire a lawyer, hire a good writer. It's not truth that will triumph, but the most coherent, credible, beautiful story. In other words, the story with the most mythical resonance, the one that best fits the jurors' cosmovision. The prosecution presents a piece of evidence and provides an interpretation. The defense proposes a different, innovative way of looking at the same piece of evidence. The jury must decide which one to choose. Which story, which body, which phantom to believe.

I never did write Alice a letter, and I'm happy with my decision. I could continue watching from outside, without her ever suspecting that I was there. I was most suited for the role of voyeur, and I was determined to keep playing it. I had discovered early on that I wouldn't find the answer in Alice.

An enormous number of *ertzaintzas* paraded through court. Before the microphone, they gave their agent numbers instead of their names. You could tell were they used to being at trial, undisturbed by the grimness of the case. Officers from the division of public security were the first to testify, given that they arrived first on the scene after Mélanie raised the alarm. Each officer corroborated the calm state in which they'd found the defendant, the babies' lack of vital signs, the scrupulously tidy house, the nanny's hysteria.

"When you arrived at the house, did the defendant demonstrate any awareness of what she had done?" the prosecutor asked each one, always in her unpleasant voice.

The officers all responded that yes, it seemed so, since the woman wouldn't stop repeating "now they're okay," as if she had completed a mission.

"In your experience," Basaguren countered in her cross-examination, "is that kind of composure typical in someone who has just committed homicide?"

No, it wasn't typical, said the first officer, although every case is different. Suspects are usually very nervous, the crime scene usually chaotic. It was true that in this case there was notable contrast between the acts committed and the defendant's behavior. Although a state of shock, the second officer tried to explain, could produce that kind of conduct.

"Are you insinuating that Ms. Espanet was in a state of shock?"

"I believe she was."

"Are you a psychiatrist, as well as a police officer?"

"A psychiatrist? No, no, but after so many years . . ."

"A simple yes or no is enough, thank you."

Agent 4182 fell silent and, quite satisfied, Carmela Basaguren had no further questions. But a short time later, the two psychiatrists who initially treated Alice at the Santiago Hospital did confirm the patient's state of shock. Disorientation, amnesia, denial of reality . . . for the duration of her time in the hospital, Alice had shown all the typical symptoms.

But the trial's lengthiest testimony came from the psychiatrist who had been treating Alice over the course of the past year. He was a Belgian physician of a certain age, with silver hair and a slew of titles and honors to his name. Entirely respectable. Doctor Leclercq. He had been based in Barcelona for many years, but his sessions with Alice were carried out in French. At Carmela Basaguren's request, all of us present were treated to a master class on postpartum depression and psychosis, a field in which he had undertaken pioneering research in the 1970s, back in his own country.

The most common manifestation is what we call the "baby blues." Eighty percent of new mothers report experiencing it, but the condition isn't considered pathological. It's caused by the hormonal imbalance of the immediate postpartum period; fatigue and lack of sleep aggravate it. But, after a few weeks, it usually disappears on its own. What are the symptoms? It is a phase marked by sadness; the new mother may cry for no apparent reason or feel overwhelmed by her situation: *I'm not cut out for this, it's too much* ... Anxiety and guilt are also very common. But, as I said, the patient generally returns to a healthy emotional balance after a few weeks. If after two or three months the situation persists or gets worse, then it's time to take measures. Good medical care includes an analysis of the patient's medical history, an examination of the mother's psychosocial state, as well as a decent number of tests to rule out potential physical causes. Now we're talking about clinical "postpartum depression," and that's no joke. Treatment usually includes a combination of psychotropic drugs and therapy—it's not a condition that's easily cured. It might take the woman years to fully recover. And it can get even worse: the clinical profile can veer into postpartum psychosis. These situations frequently include a real risk that the woman will hurt herself or harm her child, and therefore tend to require immediate hospitalization with twenty-four-hour care.

When asked by Carmela Basaguren why her client hadn't disclosed her condition to a doctor, the psychiatrist's answer was unequivocal. Sadly, Alice's situation was all too common. Various studies in Europe and the United States indicate that only a small percentage of mothers actually seek help for their postpartum depression, somewhere around 15 percent.

"This illness is still taboo today," said Dr. Leclercq. "We can't ignore the societal pressure on mothers. For the majority of women, it's very difficult to admit to themselves, to their families, to authorities (physicians are authorities, after all) that motherhood doesn't fill them with joy, and not only that, but they actually feel ruined by it."

"All the same, doctor, the path from depression to psychosis isn't a necessarily a straight one, correct?"

"That's right," said the psychiatrist. "But in Ms. Espanet's case, it's quite clear."

"You're convinced the defendant was suffering from postpartum psychosis?"

"Yes, that's correct."

"And on what do you base your diagnosis?"

"In effect, we must consider it, based on the outcome . . ." the Belgian stuttered, appearing uncomfortable for the first time during his testimony.

"Can you please be more specific?"

"As with any psychosis, this one involves losing touch with reality. At some point, a mother who is depressed may have thoughts about harming the baby, but they would be egodystonic thoughts."

"Egodystonic?" Carmela Basaguren asked with what appeared to be genuine curiosity, as if she weren't already perfectly aware of its meaning.

"That is, she might feel the impulse, but that impulse is in direct conflict with her way of thinking, which in turn produces a kind of dissonance that fills her with anxiety and guilt. But if the patient is suffering from psychosis and thinks about harming the baby, the thought won't disturb her; on the contrary, she might see clearly that it's what she has to do. Then we're talking about egosyntonic thoughts. Therefore, in an acute stage, it isn't unusual for her to go through with the impulse."

"I understand, but what makes you think that, at that moment, Ms. Espanet was suffering an acute stage of her postpartum psychosis?"

"The patient's recounting of events is clear. She felt an impulse and, instead of resisting, she went along with it."

Then the prosecutor stood for the cross-examination, the sign that this face-to-face was about to get serious. She even managed to deepen her voice. It was her moment, and she knew it. This witness could decide the case.

"Can a patient's medical history help predict postpartum psychosis?"

"It is certainly a factor to take into account."

"For example?"

"We know, for example, that patients with a history of bipolar disorder are at very high risk."

"And what does Ms. Espanet's psychiatric history tell us?"

"She has no such thing."

"She doesn't suffer from bipolar disorder?"

"No, she doesn't have a psychiatric history."

"So, Ms. Espanet's mental health was good prior to the murders?"

"That's not what I said, not at all. But she'd never been through . . . the system."

"Because nothing suggested that she had problems."

"No, no, no, those are two very different things. It's one thing for her to have never spent time in a psychiatrist's office and quite another . . . Look, when she talks about her past, the patient herself refers to bouts of bulimia and depression."

"That's what she says. But there's nothing to prove it. No official diagnosis, shall we say."

"No, but those disorders are consistent with my recent assessments."

"Okay, doctor, just to be clear. You base your diagnosis of post-partum psychosis on the defendant's behavior and her *own* accounts, is that correct?" The prosecutor unfurled this last question slowly, savoring the moment, certain that the very question contained the answer. But the Belgian psychiatrist replied as calmly to this question as he had the others.

"That's right. What else could there be? What more would you need?"

To the prosecutor's great disappointment, most of the jurors, perhaps involuntarily, nodded in agreement.

The Belgian left the stand, but the prosecution had no intention of giving up that juicy bone. Next, she called two of her own experts, the psychiatrists who had examined Alice after the events on the orders of the examining magistrate. They came to respond to the Belgian, to put the ball back in his court. Because they'd found no hint of postpartum psychosis in Alice, not even signs of depression. Postpartum psychosis, they explained, occurs in the weeks immediately following childbirth, not ten months later. This fact alone was enough to raise serious doubts. They were kind enough to give detailed descriptions of recent cases of infanticide where post-partum psychosis *had* been diagnosed, just to give us an idea. In a town in Toledo, with a ham-carving knife, a five-week-old. In Girona, a mother jumps off a balcony, her three-month old in her arms. In Madrid, a ten-day old, also in the bath. Etcetera.

Carmela Basaguren was quick to object, with possibly good reason. "I don't see how these stories are relevant. Let's stick to my client's case, shall we?"

So they did. In the most impersonal possible way, which condemned them to spectacular failure. As if reading from an academic paper, they began by mentioning Beck's Depression Inventory and the Edinburgh Postnatal Depression Scale. Following this barrage of information, in an incredibly clumsy move, they went on to read a list of Alice's psychological characteristics straight from their notes: narcissism, histrionic tendencies, propensity for victimization, constant demand for attention, self-aggrandizement, low empathy, the tendency to idealize a few people and dismiss the rest.

By that point, they'd already lost the jurors' favor: one was trying to remember when the clocks changed; another was telling herself she was ready to be a vegan once the trial was over; a third was starting to notice Carmela Basaguren's veiled sex appeal. None of the jurors were paying attention when one of the experts finally went off script and, with genuineness that trumped professionalism, said:

"Rather than a disorder, we're talking about her very nature. She's capable of committing evil, like almost everybody; but, unlike the majority, she is perfectly capable of living with it."

I called my mother that night. We normally adhere to an absurd choreography in which, if I call her, I prefer she not pick up, that way, the ball's in her court and when she calls me back, I can choose whether I want to answer, not answer, or answer just to proudly say that I'm terribly busy and we'll have to talk later. But that's not what I'm after this time. This time, I genuinely need to hear her voice.

It annoys me to acknowledge just how hard it normally is for my mother to ask about Erik; she tends to ask out of duty and then only at the end of our conversation; she tells me to send pictures, but I know she isn't genuinely interested: she's just following a social convention she read about somewhere. I send them anyway, tons of pictures, boy in a variety of poses and outfits, boy in the striped sweater she gave him. I feel pretty stupid, thinking about how many seconds she'll spend on each photo, wearily swiping her finger across the phone screen, *god how many did she send, they never end.*

But I don't want to talk to her about Erik today. Any other topic will do just fine. Her most recent boyfriend, tantric sex, her various theories about money. Only when discussing things completely unrelated to mothers does my own have charisma and light. Only then is she loveable. If I lead her toward dangerous maternal terrain, she dims, switches off. Then I'm inundated with memories of my own childhood and I make sense of them: Mother's boredom when helping me pick up toys strewn about the living room, the grimace of disgust as she wiped my boogers, her strained, exhausted expression when my father brought me back to her house on Sundays—*her* house, which I fondly thought of as *ours*; her blank stare as we amble through the aisles in the grocery store, me always asking for things, these cookies, mama, this colored macaroni, please, and my mother, deaf, mute, blind, trudging up the hill of her despair, pushing the shopping cart with me inside.

She answers on the second ring.

How am I, she's fine, just home from her pranayama class. I tell her about what I'm writing, a new project already in full swing, a kind of *noir* novel, a legal thriller. She takes my word for it since she couldn't care less about the writer side of me. I suspect she only skimmed my previous novel, having barely mentioned it to me. How are things with Niclas? she asks. Are you two still connecting in bed? I don't know why my mother thinks we ever "connected in bed." It's feels presumptuous for her to ask. Please, mother, don't you remember what it's like to have a little kid in the house? No, she doesn't remember. I tell her, as if it were a joke, that we don't have so much a sex life as a sex anecdote. Better times will come, she replies. Why don't we come to the island for Christmas and leave the baby with my father? She can sign us up for a seminar on personal erotic growth, she says.

Sometimes I think she's joking, but then I remember that she's incapable of such a thing. Everything she says, she says for real. When I was eighteen, my mother announced she was leaving. Are you kidding? She wasn't. She would let me stay in the apartment while I finished university, even until I found a job. Off she went to Lanzarote. It was true, she was leaving, she would be living at a meditation retreat center, she would work there and grow as a person. I was already grown up, I'd just turned eighteen, I didn't need a mother. Besides, my father was around, he'd be there in case of an emergency; but in short, nothing was going to happen, eighteen years old already, an adult.

I don't think I've forgiven her, but it's also true that—if she were to come back now—I wouldn't know what to do with her.

I ask her for the exact dates of the erotic growth seminar. We say our cordial goodbyes. Send me a picture of the baby. I'm on it, Mother.

It soon became apparent to me that the forensic evidence would be irrelevant, as it didn't add much to my story: those details shed light on the crime in all its simplicity, but not the phantom in all its rawness. The home security cameras quashed any possible mystery: no one else had entered the house at the time of the events. The autopsy confirmed that the children drowned in the tub, the water samples matched. A cakewalk for the forensic investigators. Even so, it never paid to drop one's guard, a lot was at stake. I, as a follower of the conventional wisdom that the Devil is in the details, tried to absorb all the explanations, no matter how repetitive or superfluous they appeared.

Ertzaintzas from the New Technologies Division showed us photos recovered from Alice's phone and computer. Several had been leaked to the press already and didn't elicit much of a reaction in the courtroom. They were of two babies dressed in classic-style clothing, chubby, not especially pretty, well-cared for at least, maybe even loved. Thousands of photos had been found. Many taken at home on her phone, but there were professional studio portraits as well. The boy was always smiling, the girl more serious.

We had to view the bathtub, there was no choice: a green plastic basin with a mustachioed cartoon seal on one of the sides. The court placed the murder weapon on a cart and wheeled it around the chamber, showing it first to the forensic police, then to the members of the jury. It was the most was tragicomic moment of the trial: the seal, the assistant's plastic gloves, the interest of some members of the jury who craned their necks for a better look, and the shadow of the exterminated babies.

The testimony of the forensic pathologists, two gloomy men, was even more painful. They brought photos. They elaborated too much. And in the end, all they did was confirm what everyone already knew. My uneasiness was so severe that I barely took notes on their testimony and now I don't have much more to say.

They were Alex and Angela, names apt for the global world, since their futures were sure to hold German summer camps, Swiss boarding schools, and later, a sufficiently prestigious university in the United Kingdom or the United States. Alex and Angela. The prosecutor was the first person to speak their names and I realized then that I'd never had that piece of information, never even noticed it was missing. They were the kids, the babies, the twins, the bodies, the ashes. It had been better like that. It was harder with the names.

Alex and Angela. A Basque paternal surname first, then their French mother's. Born in such-and-such a year, dead the next. Alex and Angela, names on the prosecutor's lips, and not even very often. After all, they were just kids.

I would spend the afternoon in the park. Although I was surrounded by other mothers willing to chat about almost any topic, I didn't want to talk to anybody. If it was raining, I went to a café that set aside a corner with a rug and a few toys to occupy the kids while the adults drank coffee. But whether I was at the park or in the baby-friendly café, I was always somewhere else in spirit: the courthouse, the chalet in Armentia, the bistro in Bordeaux where it all began.

At night, as Erik slept, I would use Niclas as a notepad, a wall, an easy mark for my obsession. I tried to write on him, bounce

114

things off him, taint his innocent soul even just a little bit.

"So, what do you think?"

"Well, that she's sick, obviously."

And if I kept asking, writing, bouncing, tainting:

"Can't we talk about something else?"

But the truth was we couldn't, and not just because of the trial. We'd long since run out of topics of conversation apart from the child-rearing venture at hand. Once we'd relayed the relevant information—today he pooped in the tub, today he coughed so hard he threw up—we'd be empty-handed and eventually I brought up the trial. Did couples really survive after raising children together? How did they manage?

"They were named Alex and Angela. Did you know?"

"How exactly would I know something like that?"

The squabble wouldn't last long. I would retreat to my corner, to my computer, and leave Niclas hooked on the latest TV series. I would open the file containing my novel and confirm that the manuscript hadn't reproduced by itself, that it was exactly as I'd left it. Then I would add in the day's notes.

I was eager for the trial to end, I thought I had enough. The live trial theater wasn't turning out to be as illuminating as I'd hoped. Very much to the contrary, it added new and increasingly inaccessible gray areas.

One of those days, as if by magic, Erik slept ten hours in a row for the first time. Two days later, the miracle occurred again, and once again a little later, a glimmer of a trend. It was an event that reminded me of winter's first snow: a silent phenomenon, discreet and elegant. When I opened my eyes the morning after a night of uninterrupted sleep, my sense was one of surprise, and I found the scene surrounding me so lovely that I believed I was somewhere else, somewhere similar to my domestic environs, but better. In that period, I only nursed him once a day, at night, to help him sleep. Things were changing, even if I couldn't see it.

She had planned it, of course. She chose a Thursday afternoon, the nanny's only day off. Her husband was out of town, as well. She gave them each half a pear mashed with a fork, then a bit of bottle. This was the last thing they ate, the autopsy confirmed. She removed their clothes. She left one of them on the floor (the boy?) while she drowned the first one. It took only a minute. She left the dead baby (the girl?) on the bed and picked up the second child. By then, she was already an expert at drowning children.

The truth is, we'll never know who she killed first. Alice has always claimed not to remember. The pathologists can only confirm they both died around the same time. Who cares whether she was controlled by ego-syntonic or ego-dystonic thoughts? What could the Beck or Edinburgh inventories possibly reveal? They're just words. Black stains on white paper.

I didn't always watch made-for-TV movies. Sometimes there was an afternoon programming miracle and they showed something that made my world stand still, even with my father snoring away next to me on the couch. I have the image of Marcello Mastroianni holding a garden hose and talking with Jack Lemmon in the twilight of their lives. Death itself does not exist, says the Italian. Does it erase what a man has done in life? Does it erase his achievements, his legacy? No. So then, Death, what are you? You are nothing. You'd like to be as important as life, but life lasts a lifetime, my friend. And you, Death, last only an instant, the instant you arrive.

What a revelation, what an urge to pick up my green Pilot pen and write down Marcello's glittering truth in my little notebook of deep, teenage thoughts.

And now I'm here, at a trial. My hands hold a different notebook and I realize now that what *caro* Marcello said in Scola's gorgeous film isn't always true. When a small child dies, murdered by family no less, it is death that prevails: life doesn't matter. It is death that lingers, death the only legacy. Death is what will be remembered, if anything. Not life. Because life was never given a chance. Only death has shone.

Another Italian film, one I watched at university in a History of Film elective. *Rome, Open City*. Roberto Rossellini's masterpiece that launched Italian Neorealism. In the final scene, the Nazis are going to shoot Don Pietro, the priest. He's helped the partisans, he's a hero; like the rest of the partisans, heroes all, he has borne Nazi torture without betraying his companions. Another priest comes over to comfort Don Pietro in his final moments. But Don Pietro faces the end with astonishing calm and dignity. It is not difficult to die well, he says in what will be the film's last dialogue, what is difficult is living a good life. They execute him while he is seated in a chair. Then the SS officer approaches and delivers the coup de grâce. The end. A good life, given for a good cause. When death has meaning.

On the flipside, and without leaving the realm of Italian cinema, we have Bertolucci's extraordinarily long *1900*. Attila Mellanchini, the histrionic fascist played by Donald Sutherland, meets his lover for an afternoon of love and play. Then little Patrizio, an Attila fan, bursts into the room. The couple incorporates the child into their sex games at first, but quickly tire of him. Attila grabs the boy by the legs, howling with laughter, and starts to spin him around and around; the boy's head smashes against the wall, the furniture, soon there's barely any head left. A short life. An atrocious death. Completely meaningless.

Their names were Alex and Angela. Angela and Alex. If they had been given time, they could have become something in life: acrobats, dentists, high-heel shoe enthusiasts, members of the Socialist party, social documentary filmmakers, museum or film library directors, professional layabouts, oboe players, unsupported artists, serious ski instructors, Euro Parliamentarians, climate change deniers, black sheep in a white family. Given a little time, they would have come to adopt an array of habits: to live aided by cocaine, defraud tax officials, wake up and read their daily horoscope, talk to strangers in bars, practice an exotic religion, make their own pasta with an appliance bought online, dance naked in front of the mirror, hate their mother and worship their father. Clumsy lovers, porn fans, loners, partiers, depressives, optimists, workers, altruists. They might have been clean, obsessive, or too lax. People who run around, their tongues hanging out, people who make a real effort to get out of bed, or who never want to sleep, hustlers, suicides, gambling addicts, beloveds, people who live off their relatives, parents of large families, contented grandparents to a pack of noisy grandkids.

In fact, there's no way to know.

8.

JUXTA CRUCEM LACRIMOSA

What is the wound of childbirth?
Roasted apple and red wine.

Anonymous, funeral song of Milia of Lastur (Fifteenth century)

One night, Alice dreamed her C-section scar was coming open. The first thing she felt was something scratching her from the inside, a faint tickle that grew into a persistent burn. Then, in terrible pain, she could see the wound opening: the freshly-stitched, viscous flesh tearing apart, seeping blood. She tried in vain to close the wound with her own hands. Her flesh had a will of its own, it was a volcano, an angry, supernatural hunk of tissue, a cataclysm. The worst came later, when the hemorrhage started to let up. From that hot pulp began to emerge a spider's leg, a leg that grabbled blindly, looking for light, and then another leg, and another. Long, hairy spider's legs, a tremulous mess, so many that she had to stop looking, suffocated by her own screams.

It wasn't a dream.

That is, they wanted to believe it was a dream, but Alice was awake, just out of the shower, about to put on her nightgown after applying rosehip oil to her scar. When Ritxi entered the bathroom, he found her clutching her abdomen, screaming in despair.

According to Ritxi's court testimony, he gave her a light tranquilizer and brought her to bed. He convinced himself it had been a dream, and assured his wife of the same. The nanny had also heard the screams, also assumed it was probably nothing, also chose to let it slide, just like everything else.

I remember another dream. And Alice appears in it again. The story is rather simple. The woman is laughing right in my face, too close. I punch her in the nose, but her nose collapses too easily, like it's an empty yogurt container. I throw in the towel. There's no way to hurt her.

The defense considered it appropriate to recount the details of Alice's labor and delivery. To that end, the gynecologist and midwives present for the birth came to testify, and a perinatal psychiatrist was called as an expert witness. She was tasked with going through some of the ins and outs of neurobiology and neuroendocrinology, as well as advances made in attachment theory. Another master class.

Alice gave birth by planned Cesarean early in her thirty-seventh week, because one of the babies—the girl—was breach, as well as cutting it close on amniotic fluid. At the appointed time, Alice showed up at the clinic, where she undressed, was anesthetized, and had the two babies removed from her womb. Afterward, they were taken away. Alice had to stay in the recovery room; she felt poorly, her blood pressure plummeted. She began to shake, unable to move her hands because of the anesthesia. I can't, she mumbled, in tears, I can't. She was thirstier than she'd ever been in her life but wasn't allowed to drink water until the effects of the anesthesia wore off. Ritxi wiped her tongue and gums with Q-tips dipped in lemon juice that barely gave her any relief. She knew nothing about the babies, she hadn't even seen them or heard if they were okay, and she didn't have the strength to ask, her voice wouldn't come out even if she tried. An hour passed and still she was still shaking, with her immobilized hands on her chest.

· As for the babies, the boy was out in an incubator, born with low birth weight, hypoglycemia, low platelet count, and respiratory distress. The girl was fine; but as a precaution, she spent the day in the NICU, too.

According to the psychiatrist, one shouldn't underestimate the effects of those hostile first hours. For one thing, a scheduled C-section bypassed a basic neurobiological process, and the massive secretion of oxytocin—that healing, magical hormone—was lost forever. For another, in deliveries like Alice's, hormonal imprinting and attachment bonding were sidestepped. This could have long-term effects: the mother could experience intense detachment from the child, with lifelong consequences for the baby. With a lump in my throat, I remembered the hours Erik and I had been separated, and decided to believe the psychiatrist's words were a bit alarmist. I never felt said alienation, bonding was immediate once he left the NICU. Besides, I had my own mother and me as counterexample: together from the beginning, yet strangers always.

The psychiatrist was an engaging speaker, in any case. She was a scientist, but she knew how to share information, and what she said was based on recent data. The jury loved her.

The separation, moreover, had made breastfeeding difficult to the point of impossible. Without stimulation from the babies, Alice never really produced milk. Each morning, a midwife came by her room and, with stubborn professionalism and using either a diabolic machine or her own fingers, squeezed Alice's nipples to the point when she shrieked in pain. On the third day, when— according to the midwife—her milk was about to come in, Alice said she couldn't take any more and asked the midwife not to come back. She could no longer bear the cruel pinches, nor the midwife's disappointed face, all for four yellowish drops. The babies would do marvelously on formula. She knew there was a pill to stop breast milk: where was the pill?

This is how they do a C-section.

The woman is anesthetized, normally only from the chest down, so she's awake throughout the whole procedure. Oftentimes, she is placed with her arms spread out and her wrists restrained. She's given an IV. Her vital signs are monitored. A catheter is inserted into her urethra to keep her bladder empty at all times. Another tube goes in her nose to provide supplemental oxygen.

Her abdomen and upper pubic area are shaved. The skin is disinfected. Then the doctor asks for the scalpel. The first cut: the laparotomy, a transverse incision some fifteen centimeters long in the lower abdomen. (The transverse incision is an innovation in the history of the Cesarean, and it has one inarguable advantage: a bikini will hide the scar). Following that first incision, the layer of fatty tissue is pulled back and the connective tissue that holds the muscles of the abdomen (the *aponeurosis*) is cut horizontally, usually with scissors. Then the abdominal muscles are pulled apart by hand and the peritoneum, the thin tissue that covers most of the internal organs in the abdomen, is cut.

After this excavation, the treasure chest, the uterus, appears and now comes the second slice with the scalpel: the hysterotomy. All that's left is to rupture the amniotic sac and, after draining any remaining fluid, take the baby out. The umbilical cord is then cut and the placenta manually removed.

Now it's time to stitch all the incisions, tracing the steps backward. First the uterus. They don't touch the peritoneum, it will heal on its own. The aponeurosis is sutured. Lastly, the skin is closed, often with staples.

The whole surgery lasts about an hour. The body absorbs the

uterine sutures in forty days. Localized pain may last for months.
There are other complications that can persist for life: injury to
the adjacent organs, organs that remain stuck together, difficulty
or impossibility of getting pregnant again.

Contrary to popular belief, Julius Caesar was not born by
Cesarean. His mother, Aurelia, lived to be sixty-six and, until
the twentieth century, all women (with one or two documented
exceptions) who underwent a Cesarean died as a result, if not
from the immediate hemorrhaging, then from infection a few
days later.

Something happened when they left the hospital. Ritxi and Alice
drove home with Angela. They'd had to leave Alex, who was still
admitted. Alice sat in back with the baby. It was a short drive, not
even fifteen minutes. Ritxi was nervous but elated; he was making
plans, designing the hours ahead. But Alice seemed downcast,
two dark circles under her eyes punctuated by a dull, grayish face.
Probably because she'd had to leave the boy behind, the husband
thought. But surely they'd all be together soon, and besides, they
would see him back at the hospital that afternoon. Alice met
Ritxi's effusion with defiant silence. Finally, he decided to stop
talking and turned on the radio: classical, Fauré's *Requiem*. He was
also exhausted and had to accept that all his euphoria was largely
artificial. Then he stopped at a red light and suddenly, without
warning, Alice undid the baby's straps and her own seatbelt and
got out of the car, the baby in her arms. Ritxi froze, he hadn't a
clue as to what was happening and sat waiting, perhaps, for some
sign. The light turned green. Accustomed as he was to obeying
traffic signals, his situation was certainly unnerving. The horns
honking behind him, pressuring him to move on, didn't help. He
wound up ditching the car as well, and saw his wife sheltering in
a doorway, singing the baby a lullaby.

"What are you doing, Alice?"

"We can't stay in that car," she said placidly. "The fumes will kill her."

"What fumes? What are you talking about?"

"The gas fumes."

It took him almost five minutes to convince her there were no fumes inside the car: the baby was fine, they were all fine. Alice didn't seem nervous, just stubborn, convinced. Ritxi had to promise that they'd keep the windows down the whole way, and also had to deal with the two cops who'd come to investigate the cause of the mounting traffic chaos. Ritxi assured them it was taken care of, they were moving on, it had all been a misunderstanding. The officers looked at the newborn and decided to let them go. At last, Ritxi and Alice left.

They didn't speak the rest of the drive. The baby started to cry and Alice spent the whole time trying to soothe her with a pacifier, which Angela refused to take. Once home, there was so much to do, and they were so preoccupied with the newborn that they never discussed the incident.

But hadn't his alarm bells gone off? Weren't there enough reasons for him to seek help?

Ritxi rubbed between his brows, breathed heavily, stammered into the microphone.

Of course. That's why they hired Mélanie, to lighten the workload. That's why a reiki master came to their house, to relieve his wife's chronic sadness. Why she went to Pilates, two classes a week. And the general sense was that things were improving. The situation seemed under control.

Had it been enough? In hindsight, no. But what could Ritxi do now? What?

(By the way, there is no municipal police record of the traffic incident Ritxi described, as was shown in court).

Of the witnesses, Mélanie the au pair was the only one to testify behind a screen. She refused a court interpreter, but was incapable of facing Alice. It was a point in the prosecution's favor, surely, as that stage prop dramatized the danger posed by Alice, her evilness, the need for protection from all of that.

Yet, on the other hand, Mélanie's explanations suggested that Alice wasn't right in the head, so the question that remained was about the extent of her madness, and how far that madness might go in explaining, or even pardoning, her criminal acts.

How long had Mélanie worked in Alice and Ritxi's home? Since the babies were a month old until . . . well, until the end. Had Mélanie liked working there? Not really. Why not? The young woman didn't hesitate: because of the mother. You couldn't predict her behavior. Sometimes she would spend the whole day breathing down Mélanie's neck, supervising her every move, telling her how to hold the babies, how to change their diapers or apply lotion. Other times, she clapped her hands and bid Mélanie a merry adieu and locked herself in her studio—to paint, she said—leaving everything to Mélanie. The nanny preferred the latter, of course, despite the work. The days that Alice was all over her, her mood was erratic: either she'd be grumbling, criticizing the nanny's every move, or depressed, discouraged because the babies weren't gaining weight or they looked too fat or they hardly slept or their naps were too long, they weren't sick, were they? What was wrong with them?

Anything else unusual, besides that?

Well, yes. Sometimes Alice burst into whatever room Mélanie was in to announce, panic-stricken, that she had lost the children. At first, the nanny would be just as dismayed as the mother and stop whatever she was doing to run to the twins' bedroom where, to her relief, she would find them napping, right where she'd left them five minutes earlier. This episode was repeated four or five times, until Mélanie began to simply ignore Alice or mollify her dismissively. They're not lost, Alice, they're in their room, go and see, just don't wake them, please.

If only she had taken all of that more seriously . . .

If she'd at least spoken to the father . . .

But it's just that the father, well, the father was hardly ever home, and when he was, he barely acknowledged Mélanie's existence.

If only she hadn't gone out that afternoon with that boy she'd just met . . .

But it was her only free afternoon. And he was the first guy to ask her out since she'd moved to the city.

"In your opinion, did Alice love her children?" asked Carmela Basaguren, with a forthrightness that—to my ear—rang false.

"She worried about them a lot. If that's love . . ."

Mélanie finished her testimony in tears, and the two jurors most inclined to show emotion discreetly wiped their eyes.

"She won't get off, you know that, right?"

Someone was speaking to me on my left, someone who, like me, was bellied up to the bar, having a coffee and *pintxo* of potato omelet.

"Excuse me?"

"No matter how hard her lawyer works it, the Frenchwoman will end up behind bars."

"Oh."

"Sorry, it's just that I see you in court every day, I thought you'd noticed me, too. Guess not."

I was at a loss for words. The truth was, I *had* noticed him, the journalist who always sat in the front row, who was so tan he looked Indian, slender as a ballet dancer, so handsome that, if he ever spoke to me, I would be lucky to manage a stutter. Which was exactly what was happening.

"You're not a journalist, are you?"

"No, no . . . I'm here for research."

"Ah, from the university."

I didn't try to correct him, but I didn't exactly feel like I was lying, either.

"When there are no doubts about a case, when the accused has been caught *in fraganti* or makes a clear confession, the lawyers have just one card they can play. The insanity defense. And they'll always find a psychiatrist willing to play along. Ego-syntonic, ego-whatever, imprinting . . . like we were ducklings. They must be really desperate, trotting out all that rubbish. I'm Jakes, by the way."

He mentioned the newspaper he worked for. "So, you're not from India?" I felt compelled to ask. Fortunately, I reined myself in.

"All the same, this case is pretty special. A mother, her own kids . . ." I would say anything to keep talking.

"Happens more often than you think. Actually, we're all more likely to be killed by a family member than a stranger."

"And the defendant's profile, I meant," I added, even though my body was begging me to be in complete agreement with that man.

"Ah, yes . . . foreign, rich, full support of the husband . . . Not exactly a desperate woman of the lumpen class."

"And absolutely gorgeous."

"That too. But with this jury, she doesn't stand a chance."

"How come?"

"Most of them are women, you know. And add on your typical cruelty with these types of juries. Did you know that the conviction rate is much higher with trial juries? Give them a little power and your average citizen turns merciless."

Oh, Jakes, why didn't you come over on the first day? Why do you speak to me now, on the penultimate day of the trial, just as I'm grabbing my coat and hat and ditching this party? You had so many interesting things to share! But now that you're in my orbit, I won't let you move away so easily.

"But you personally, what do you think? Why did she do it?" I asked.

"Because she realized she didn't want children. She didn't want them, they bothered her. She wanted to get rid of that burden, thinking she had every right to. But most of all, because she's a cold-hearted witch incapable of love."

"That simple?"

"Why not? Sometimes that's all there is."

A father has dinner with his family. Lasagna and yogurt. Then they all watch a show together. Some zany competition. Like every other night, the father kisses his six- and eight-year-old daughters, asleep in their bunk beds. Then he kisses his wife's neck as she applies anti-aging cream, and they talk over their plans for the next day. Later, he closes himself in his study, takes out the pistol he keeps in a locked drawer, and puts it in his mouth. Bang. No goodbye note. The pistol is the message.

Sometimes it happens. It's a real story, the father of one of my classmates. That simple. There are those who draw near the soul's abyss so often that in the end they succumb to one of two impulses: jump in themselves or shove the person beside them. The death drive. The biggest hit of power you can take. The power to end it all. Something that can be brought about so simply, so easily and quickly and efficiently, that once it's done, a feeling of disbelief prevails over guilt or regret.

I would have liked to tell Jakes about this, but I was incapable of articulating grand ideas in front of him.

"Okay, maybe you're right," I said instead. "Humans can be like that, but, but . . ."

"But but but. Better leave the rhetorical sleights to the defense. Shall we go back in? Recess is over," Jakes grinned. I was already swooning.

"Yeah, let's go."

There's a big hole in Alice's biography that no one seems willing or interested in filling. Thanks to Léa, I have some idea of the kind of life Alice led until she was twenty-one or twenty-two. At trial, her marriage, infertility treatments, and conflicted motherhood have been under the microscope. But in the middle, there is a three- or four-year period during which time the woman disappears off the radar and at least one notable thing occurs: the name change. Jade dies and Alice is born. Why? Because *Jade didn't fit the social class she aspired to, because she wanted to rebel against her mother, who knows*, Léa said when I asked her on Telegram. She didn't think it was very important. Alice had kept her mother's surname, Espanet. That didn't mean much to my friend, either.

Two months after they met in Bordeaux, Alice had settled in Vitoria. Her weekend visits had become week-long ones and soon, almost imperceptibly, the woman had moved all her belongings into Ritxi's penthouse in the city center. Those belongings consisted of one suitcase full of makeup and another filled with clothes. Ritxi introduced his girlfriend to his friends over a dinner he organized at his supper club. His friends don't remember much about that dinner. A beautiful, discreet young woman. Pretty much what they expected. They weren't surprised to receive wedding invitations a few months later. They did what they always did in such cases and planned a bachelor party for Ritxi. Weekend in Ibiza, rented sailboat, case of Veuve Clicquot and a nice sampling of other drugs better left unmentioned in court. Moreover, they convinced their wives and girlfriends to take Alice out for her own pre-wedding celebration. Grudgingly, out of obligation, the female division of the friend group went to find the mysterious Frenchwoman (yes, she was mysterious, they admit) and take her to brunch at the only hotel in Vitoria that served it in those days. Then they spent the afternoon at a spa, getting Iong Bao massages.

Alice had no close friends among them, but they had treated

her nicely, claimed the woman who acted as spokesperson for the others at the trial. It was Alice who insisted on keeping her distance, Alice who declined to take part in conversations, Alice who replied to every question with a sardonic smile. She never came right out and said it, but Alice had hinted that she'd suffered in life and that's why she looked down on them, that bunch of spoiled daddy's girls, healthy, endogamous women whose lives had always been cushy.

What they couldn't understand—the witness spoke in the plural, emphasizing the tribal nature of their group—was how Alice could be so unappreciative. In spite of the fact that she came from who-knows-where, Alice had been warmly accepted into the upper echelons, simply because one fine day a man laid eyes on her and liked what he saw so much that he decided to keep her. The witness put it differently, but that was the gist, more or less. And now that Alice knew all the passwords that offered access to their privileged world, all she did was wrinkle her nose and make disparaging comments every time one of them congratulated herself on the success of her fashion blog, or when another tearfully recounted the dramatic ongoing conflict with the interior designer redoing her living room and kitchen.

The truth is that they barely saw Alice, only at certain social commitments and little else. One of the last occasions had been the twins' baby shower, just before they were born. They always celebrated with a shower when one of them was pregnant, and they'd seen no way to break from tradition in Alice's case. It was held on a rainy day at the chalet in Armentia, where they were all surprised to see Alice drinking wine (two glasses, at least, and not even from her own husband's label!) and going on and on about the mortal dangers of pregnancy and childbirth. She had memorized the horrid statistics, according to which 4.7 out of every 1,000 babies born in the Basque Autonomous Community died in childbirth or shortly thereafter. She seemed convinced her twins wouldn't survive the ordeal, and that's why, the women assumed, Alice set aside each opened gift (video monitors, an ergonomic baby carrier, a nightlight projector) with impassive indifference.

No, they didn't like Alice, but deep down they were grateful for the chance to gossip with solid reasons to talk badly about someone. They couldn't deny that she had supplied them with many an hour of catty entertainment and backstabbing. Alice had become the unwitting protagonist of many a whispered phone conversation and much stifled laughter. The witness didn't say this last part, but that was my impression. I wrote it down.

"What a terrible impression that snob made," Jakes said after the session, when I was already rushing out, car keys in hand.

"You think so?" Unconsciously, I returned the keys to my purse. "What she said didn't make Alice look very good, either."

"Yeah, but whose side do you want to take? The plastic Barbie who spends her time and her husband's money on three-thousand-euro purses and exotic-sounding massages, or deep, mysterious, tragic Alice?"

"Well, honestly she didn't exactly pick the best outfit to appear before a judge. Those heels . . ."

"Chanel booties."

"Right."

(Did this man know everything?)

"Hey, I'm starving, want to get something to eat? You still haven't told me about this research of yours."

He threw out the invitation casually, no big deal, and my heart started to dance. Still, I reacted quickly, led by my basest instinct: good sense.

"I can't today. I have to get back to Bilbao."

I didn't specify why, or with whom I'd be spending the afternoon.

"Too bad."

"Tomorrow?"

"Tomorrow's the last day."

"Exactly, we can celebrate."

"All right." He stuck out his hand and we shook on it. I was trembling. I'm not sure if he noticed.

I started talking to myself on the highway, something I do only when very drunk or very nervous.

Hey hey, just what are you up to? Fuck, it's a date, isn't it?

How could it be a date? It's a work lunch, we'll talk about the case. He knows nothing about you, and you know nothing about him. And if he's married, then what?

You're married, too, chickie!

Exactly. Two married adults, nothing romantic to see here, move along people. Besides, isn't it odd that he knew those were Chanel booties?

What? You think he's gay? Those are old-fashioned prejudices, girl.

I didn't shut up until I hit the tolls, and inside I was still roiling. I hadn't felt that way in a long time, maybe not since I was fifteen. I had to manage the situation carefully, given that the probability of doing something stupid seemed high. More than the fact that an attractive man had noticed me, I was pleased by my own response. From the moment I got pregnant, it was like I'd been stuck in a cold, damp cave where rays of sunlight couldn't reach. And two years later, I saw myself emerging from the cave, stretching my limbs, warming up my muscles and skin, ready for a whole new range of erotic pleasures.

I had plenty of work ahead.

4.

MOTHERS' DREAMS

Why has no one come up with an equivalent of Ikea for
childcare, an equivalent of Microsoft for housework?
VIRGINIE DESPENTES, *King Kong Theory*

In fairy tales, the villain is always the stepmother, never the mother.
It's the stepmother who oppresses Cinderella. The stepmother who
wants Snow White's heart in a box. In these stories, the mother
never appears: she's long dead, forgotten. The heroine's only
mission, her only way out, is to free herself from her stepmother.

Why this obsession with stepmothers? Psychoanalysis claims
that the figure of the stepmother actually represents dissociation
in the child's mind. The mother and the stepmother are one. One
is the dark half of the other. When the mother behaves cruelly,
wickedly, she is turned into the stepmother, the other. Mother no
longer. Until she returns to the path of goodness, of tenderness,
she won't earn back her title.

This isn't just a psychological need of children.

The Judeo-Christian tradition has taken this dissociation
to absurd extremes, going so far as to invent the figure of the
virgin mother. The virgin mother isn't strictly a Judeo-Christian

invention, however: it's another mytheme, a universal narrative unit that appears independently in cultures that didn't have contact with one another. Athena, goddess of wisdom and war and one of the most important goddesses in Greek mythology, was a virgin. Hephaestus so desired her that he ejaculated on her clothing; Athena, disgusted, flung the drips of semen to the ground, from which, suddenly, Erichthonius was born. Athena made him her son, her virginity intact. Maya, the Buddha's mother, also conceived her son chastely, this time in a dream, an illumination: Buddha enters through the right side of her body, on a lotus throne carried by a white elephant. The Aztec goddess Coatlicue was peacefully sweeping a temple when a ball of beautiful feathers fell from the sky. She touched the ball and became pregnant. Shortly thereafter Huitzilopochtli, the Aztec god, would be born, conceived without sin. The Persian god Mithra was born from Anahita's belly, albeit in an unusual way (or not, I suppose), given that Anahita was a virgin.

To what do we owe this recurring obsession with virgin pregnancies? Where does it come from, this hysterical, anti-biological, anti-empirical, and frankly misogynistic, dissociation? If a woman is a mother, sex cannot interfere in her life. If she falls into the clutches of sex, she isn't a mother, she's a whore. If she's a whore, she doesn't give life; to the contrary, she's probably dangerous, capable of taking a life should anyone fall prey to her mortal snare. The woman who isn't a murderer, isn't a whore . . . *she's* the mother, giver of life.

Or to put it more simply.

All women are whores, except my mother.

We've heard that story before.

Carmela Basaguren had a special talent for telling new, refreshing stories. In this respect, she wildly outdid the prosecution. The public prosecutor had entered the battle thinking it would be a cakewalk, but without knowing exactly how it happened, she now found herself bogged down in the biblical contradictions of a murderer-mother, all dressed in psychiatric jargon that obscured things even further. I saw her wipe sweat from her brow more than once, always when the defense was on full-blown attack: psychosis, insanity, hallucinations, if not, then what, just look at her, how else can you explain it.

At any rate, the shadow of the two babies had to hang over the courtroom, I thought, somebody must be thinking of them, of their cruel end, water-logged lungs, faces tinged blue. And those hands, the mother's hands. Those hands that could have stopped, but chose to go all the way. Or were the prosecutor and I really the only ones trying to hold on to the thread connecting the babies to this world?

The wicked mother vs. the good writer. Another dissociation.

An incomplete checklist:

√   The good writer locks herself in her room and won't open the door even if her child pounds on it. If the child begs and cries, the good writer will resist. She'll wear earplugs, put another lock on the door. She's writing.

√   The good writer hires nannies to be with the child while she writes.

√   The good writer uses her motherhood as raw material for her literature, even if she can't perform a mother's functions while she writes.

√   The good writer reads books on attachment theory, the physiology of childbirth, childrearing in Ancient Greece. Her nose in a book, she doesn't see that her child has tumbled off the slide.

√   The good writer, when she holds her little cub for the first time, is already thinking about how to describe the experience in a unique way.

√ The good writer can discuss *Madame Bovary* from the perspective of gender, explaining why the woman's sexual desire and lack of maternal instinct are two sides of the same coin.

√ The good writer has even gone so far as to occasionally envy Emma Bovary, who left her newborn daughter with a wet nurse, only visiting her on some Sundays, only a few Sundays, to be honest.

√ The good writer wonders if someday her children will forgive her for being such a good writer.

√ The good writer, actually, wishes she were a man.

The atom, the grain of sand. The whole universe is contained within them. The most insignificant gesture can predict the final movement. The brief but eternal gesture, able to turn life into death. Only visible to those with a circular sense of time.

Alice never completely banished her passion for painting. Her hands were always dirty. She had her own studio in the house in Armentia. Ritxi, who had always liked that facet of his wife, encouraged her to keep it up. Alice shut herself up in her studio every day. Sometimes she produced something. In the year leading to the events, she'd given up watercolors in favor of oils and experimenting with collage. The female body continued to be a recurrent subject. Bodies increasingly deformed, broken; canvasses increasingly bloody: menstruation, birth, visible pain, red.

Ritxi suggested she paint the spider.

So Alice did. She put her C-section on the canvas, the scar coming undone, the long, hairy spider legs. The paintings kept growing in size. She made use of all kinds of material, glued on red plastic, random wrappers, wire, sharp wire that could cut flesh. She cut the hair off all the stuffed animals in the house and stuck it to the paintings. Those shaggy creatures creeping through trails of blood completely lost their spider-shape.

Ritxi was truly impressed. He didn't know much about art, but he trusted his own innate sensibility was enough for him to judge whether the work before him was important, or at least special. Those were nine powerful paintings, he was sure of it.

"We need to organize a show."

"I don't have time, the kids ..." Alice replied quickly, as if she'd already considered it.

"The kids are fine. We have Mélanie, and I'll help set it all up."

She gave in. Alice gave in readily since the day the twins were born.

The show would be held at Ritxi's winery, in the modern, elegant tasting room. They would host an opening reception, of course, and invite certain friends and acquaintances whom Ritxi had already mentally selected. A small catalog would have to be designed—his PR girl would take care of it. Naturally, the paintings would be for sale. In the 180 to 300 euro-range, depending on size. And Ritxi had even more plans. It suddenly seemed that he'd hit upon a solution for his wife's chronic sadness, and his mind was racing. Alice should design a wine label. She could use her usual motifs, although it would be good to tone down the rawness, to make it more commercial. He was sure Alice's spiders would be the perfect fit for a signature carbonic red he'd been thinking up. The wine would be called Alice, of course.

The day of the opening, Ritxi and Alice set off for La Rioja before noon, leaving the twins with Mélanie. Alice never visited her husband's workplace. She was nervous but excited. Her first show. And the first time she would be away from the babies for so long. Practically a whole day, eight or nine hours at least. She called Mélanie every thirty minutes. The nanny only answered half the time. Fed up, she finally told Alice that she was busy changing diapers, feeding the kids their fruit, she barely had time to go to the bathroom, much less answer the phone.

Everything was essentially ready by the time they arrived.

Winery staff had hung the nine paintings, selected the wine to serve to guests, and were managing the catering. The PR girl had the catalog ready, a simple brochure printed on standard-size paper and folded one by one with her own hands, eighty copies fanned out on the center table.

There was nothing left for Alice to do but fold her hands and wait. Ritxi got tied up with an urgent work matter (an unavoidable phone call), and then another (a quick meeting with the marketing director), despite his promises that he wouldn't work that day, that he would be all hers.

"Why don't you go for a walk, love? Take advantage that it's stopped raining."

It was a spring day, cold and unpleasant. The grapevines looked like charred stumps. Alice rarely went to La Rioja and now she remembered why. She didn't like that landscape; even at its peak, in the fall, she found the palette oppressive. She preferred her colors cool.

After his father's death, Ritxi had taken on the renovation of the property himself. He added a large glass block to the hundred-year-old original stone building and this annex now served as the winery's entrance. Alice decided to walk the path that ringed the old building. She would get muddy if she strayed, and she hadn't brought other shoes. She was plagued with doubts about her outfit. All black, head to toe. If only she'd brought a more colorful scarf. At that point she was overcome with a terrible headache and had to stop her uninspired meandering. She leaned against the building and lit a cigarette. She felt a shiver, and that was when she heard the words exiting through the crack of an open window.

"A cheap knock-off of Louise Bourgeois, nine times over. But who will care? Nobody, they'll all be sold in the first half an hour, everyone wanting to get in good with Ritxi. And to think I had to waste an hour of my life making a 'catalog' for that rubbish ..."

The PR girl was talking on the phone. Alice dropped her

cigarette and stepped on it with her black shoes.

When Ritxi got out of his urgent meeting a half hour later, he found his wife in the tasting room. But there weren't any paintings there now. No intact ones, anyway. Alice had taken one of the bottles of wine for the reception and bashed it viciously on the table, shattered it, and with the red-stained bottleneck slashed the canvasses, in some cases with such rage that she cracked the wooden frame. The wine, which had splattered across the walls and floor, lent the scene a touch of gore.

"The show is over," said Alice. "We're going home. I want to see the kids."

She tossed what was left of the bottle on the floor and got ready to get out of there. With a lump in his throat, Ritxi asked her to please wait for him in the car. He had to speak to his staff first, somehow explain what had happened.

But still, Ritxi did not seek help, not even after that incident. On the stand, he tried to explain why not. The PR girl—unasked— had taken photos of the massacre, and the graphic evidence showed to the jury revealed a post-apocalyptic scene. There was a lot of rage in that artistic cruelty—why hadn't he reacted?

An unflappable Ritxi shared his point of view. Was what had happened really all that strange? He didn't think so. He gave us his reasons: 1) An artist's standard but pathological dissatisfaction with his or her work (did we know that Kafka gave all his written work to a friend and asked him to burn it?); 2) The lack of confidence experienced by anyone presenting works of such an intimate nature to the public (he wasn't an artist, but he could understand it); 3) A certain degree of jealousy (here he made subtle but clear reference to the PR girl's physical attributes); and lastly, 4) The consequences, although dramatic, hadn't been all that serious, given that, in the blink of an eye, the whole mess had been wiped up (by others) with a rag and mop.

It was a studied explanation, delivered with real confidence, and Ritxi even got defensive when the prosecutor tried to suggest a relationship between the aborted art show and the crimes. What a waste of time to keep talking about the goddamn show, Ritxi's body language seemed to say.

Maybe he was right.

What do I know.

Maybe it isn't true that the essence of the whole universe is contained in a single atom. Maybe a grain of sand is just a grain of sand. And the final gesture may arrive without warning. The truth is, no one can predict which popcorn kernel will be first to pop.

Another void. We know almost nothing about Alice's life after the twins' death. What little we do know comes from interesting sources: her husband and the Belgian psychiatrist. Both speak to us of a life of withdrawn isolation. Alice barely leaves the house. She takes very strong medication. She's never alone. A nurse watches her while Ritxi is at work. She travels frequently to Barcelona, to the Belgian's practice. From car to plane, plane to cab, cab to the psychiatrist's office, and back, all on the same day. Ritxi is giving her everything: all his time, all his money, all his love. At least this last one appears to be inexhaustible. He lost his children forever, at worst he would like his wife back, the love of his life. The psychiatrist says she's getting better. But she'll need time. More therapy, more pills. And the probability of relapse will always be high. No, under no circumstances would he recommend she have more children.

But how can we be sure they're telling the truth? What Alice does or stops doing inside her home is a mystery. If she goes out, if she meets anyone, if she proposes a toast in her living room . . . we don't know. If the trial had been a private prosecution, an option provided under Spanish law in which ordinary citizens can pursue criminal charges and file criminal complaints, a private investigator would have likely followed the defendant for months, studying her behavior, documenting it, catching her in more than one lie.

But no one has bothered. There's no private prosecutor looking out for the children's interests. After all, they were just kids and almost nobody remembers them now.

I've already mentioned two of the feelings that characterized my experience of Erik's first months: exhaustion and boredom. I have yet to mention the third, although it is perhaps just as significant: fear. Why haven't I brought it up before? Because I'm embarrassed. The other feelings lend me an air of independence; with fear, I'm an ordinary mother doomed to inevitable suffering. And yet, the fear was there. Constantly. Like background music nobody knows how to turn off. Like a sweaty dance partner who holds you too close. Fear.

Having a vivid imagination is not a good thing. Maybe it's a benefit in the realm of sexual fantasies and a few other areas of minor importance. But as a quality, most of the time it just brings unpleasantness. Who could curb a first-time mother's diabolical imagination? My fear was very concrete, but its branches were endless and twisting and essentially revolved around the many ways Erik could die. For example:

He could fall off a bridge and into the estuary while I was pushing him in the stroller. Just one bump from a jogger, one foolish stumble. Would I be capable of jumping in to save him? I didn't think so, not before he was fatally sunk by the weight of the stroller.

Another fear, the most ridiculous one. I blush now, but at the time I saw it as a real possibility. I feared I would accidentally load Erik into the washing machine. Why not? It's possible. The baby would be sleeping on a blanket in a corner of the living room, and I, an automaton in my sleep-deprived fog, would be gathering dirty clothes from the floor, towels with spit-up, baby blankets, and amid the clutter, I would pick up the blanket with his little body inside, he's so very light I wouldn't even notice, and stuff him into the machine, never hearing his cries. I would press the button for the quick-wash cycle and only then realize what I had done. The clothes would start to spin, the drum would fill with water in a matter of seconds. Before the glass, like a horror film, I would witness my baby's agony and death. For months, every time I pressed the start button on the washer, a small shiver of panic ran up my spine. Anyone familiar with the ridiculous amount of laundry you do with a newborn at home will understand my state of distress.

There was more: open windows, toys the ideal size to get stuck in his throat, electrical outlets, bottles of bleach, the cord on the iron, hot oil with the tendency to spatter, and more dangers, always present, lying in wait, and detailed on the info sheet from the pediatrician's office. There was no rest.

The child's natural fate seemed to be to suffer some absurd accident. And it seemed obvious to me at the time that if someone wanted to end a child's life and spare themselves the guilt, a laissez-faire attitude would be enough: a marble in the building blocks, a chair set beside an open window, a box of detergent under the kitchen table. It was just a matter of time. Sit and wait. The perfect crime.

With two children, Alice's situation was more complicated. Two such accidents (simultaneous, or consecutive) broke all reasonable laws of probability.

We have one of Louise Bourgeois's spiders in here in Bilbao, behind the Guggenheim. The sculpture is called *Maman*. I've passed beneath its long legs on more than one of my walks with Erik. If you stop under the creature and look up, you can see eggs in a sac between its legs. It's a mother. Like me. Because for Bourgeois, the spider represents the protective web of motherhood. "Spiders make good company," the Parisian artist said in an interview. "They eat mosquitoes. They're proactive, a big help. That's how my mother was."

Bourgeois's spiders, then, are not vile creatures capable of perforating the uterus and muscling their way out, layer by layer, until, bloodied, they reach the surface.

Last day of the trial. Following this session, the jury would retire to deliberate for a day, two days, we didn't know how long. A final effort. Sit in the same seat, with the same innocent diligence as the law students and their coherent and purely pedagogical reasons for being there.

A rough three-week journey was coming to an end. A work of theater that, unlike the films of Hollywood, had been riddled with boring, repetitive bits absolutely devoid of interest. And yet, I still had the hope that if Alice should agree to make a final statement, we would reach some sort of climax.

But also.

But especially.

That was the day I would have lunch with Jakes. He was the reason I was wearing lipstick. The reason I was trembling—not my anticipation of the closing arguments. Would he remember our date? If not, would I have to remind him with practiced nonchalance? Hey, Jakes, still up for lunch? You'll have to pick the place, I don't really know this area. I wasn't sure I'd be up to it. But I'd have to be. I had told Niclas that since it was the last session, we would likely go longer than usual. Happy that the fucking trial was almost over, he didn't ask too many questions. In addition, I'd made an anomalous, last-minute arrangement with my father, who agreed to pick up Erik from daycare. It was a nice, sunny fall day, they could play contentedly at the park for two hours until I got back. With a bit of luck, he wouldn't even have to change Erik's diaper. The web of white lies and logistics involved too many people for my shyness or the dark-haired journalist to fail me now. But if things didn't work out, I was sure I'd return to Bilbao somewhat relieved, aware of having escaped the sticky spiderweb tightening around me. Sometimes I'm such a coward.

Just what were my real intentions with respect to Jakes? Truthfully, I wasn't expecting more than a pleasant lunch. A brief, harmless flirtation. A few coquettish smiles and fertilizer for future fantasies. Nothing else. Conversation would be light at first; when choosing the wine, it would be easy for me to hint that I knew a little something about it, then I'd swiftly mention my years in London (I always play that card when I sense someone's interest in me waning), and once we were on the second course, we'd finally approach the subject we had most in common: the trial and its outcome. I planned to reveal to him that I was a novelist ("Of course! I thought I recognized your face! I love your book!" the handsome reporter exclaimed in my wildest fantasies) who was writing about Alice's crime and that I had to understand why she had done it, why the Hell she had done what she'd done.

At that moment, erotic fervor and intellectual fervor were indistinguishable to me.

I sensed that the still-tenebrous aspects of Alice's case would be illuminated by talking to Jakes. I needed someone as familiar with it as I was, but who wasn't me. That's how the story would finally move forward, take the shape it deserved. All my hope lay in Jakes. There was no Plan B. He held the keys, this dark-haired man I'd met just the day before. At the time, this idea made sense and put me in a good mood. I even considered making Jakes a character and introducing him toward the end of the book.

And that was all. Nothing more, nothing less. At most, we'd share dessert: he'd have a little of my brownie, I'd try a bite of his flan. At most, I'd text Léa about it when I got home. *Slut*, she'd write. *You know what you're doing, you little tart, I've quit all that, you know. DANGER! DANGER!*

Nothing more, nothing less.

So, the last session. Maybe Alice would be transferred straight to prison from that very courtroom, maybe for the rest of her life. Highway, tolls, court, notebook filled with thoughts, all for the last time; then, at last I would start to write without a safety net. Write freely. Regain my confidence, blind faith. I'd been sacrificing a lot along the way and that could only mean that, from my fingertips, a masterpiece must flow. I was up for it, sure I was. Through writing, the crime would be revealed in all its honesty. Nothing was out of bounds. The truth would be laid bare in the frenzied rhythm of the keys. And I would understand it. And everyone would understand why I understood.

With Jakes's help.

A tally of the mother-writer's sacrifices. Another incomplete list:

- √ Relationship with her partner. Its cache of intimacy, honesty, and trust. SACRIFICED.
- √ Quality time with the child, essential for early emotional and cognitive development. SACRIFICED.
- √ Financial stability (account balance: 2,897 euros, with the book still left to write). SACRIFICED.
- √ The privilege of considering myself a good person (and not a vulture circling two drowned babies). SACRIFICED.

The prosecutor opened her closing argument with the children's names.

"They were named Alex and Angela, in case anyone's forgotten. They were human beings, like all of us. They had their whole lives ahead of them, they needed someone to love and care for them, they were unique and wonderful, like each one of us." Pause for effect, ruined by the judge's heavy breathing. "But the world, in short, isn't always what we are told. Mothers aren't always like what we've been told. A mother can be cruel. To think otherwise is to cave in to an outdated view of motherhood and femininity. A mother's cruelty needn't always go hand in hand with madness. Ladies and gentlemen, in the name of feminism, and as a woman myself, I categorically reject that idea."

I thought this last bit was a little over-the-top, mostly because she ended it with a fist pump, but I didn't withdraw my confidence in her yet.

"Evil exists. We prefer other explanations: that it's the product of social inequality or mental illness. That comforts us. We have social services and pills for that. But sometimes, evil is simply there: humanity's dark side in its purest, most distilled form. There are wicked mothers. There are mothers who consider their children their creations. Under this perverse logic, they believe they have the right to destroy what they've created. The world, after all, will be the same. The harmony of the universe will be preserved. They believe they have that divine power. This is undoubtedly the case with Alice."

For the first time since the start of the trial, Alice began doodling on the piece of paper in front of her. Her lawyer whispered and Alice stopped. Unfortunately, it was impossible from the sixth row to make out what it was she had written or drawn.

"Evil invades everything, even drowning out guilt. Few times in my career have I seen such a nasty piece of work. Because— look at her—the nastiness is followed by nothing but the most absolute indifference."

Not bad, all in all. Probably her best performance. She was speaking from a place of fury, that much was clear.

Then Carmela Basaguren got to her feet and repeated the defense's request for acquittal, citing Article 20.1 for the last time. Was it terrible, what Alice had done? It was hard for her to imagine a more horrendous act. Was it unacceptable, what had happened to those two little creatures who had deserved all the love and protection in the world? There was no doubt. But was it appropriate to lock up this broken, devastated, confused woman for life? What could be gained from that? By giving Alice a harsh sentence, would the jury feel they were doing something good? Could they go back to their homes with a clear conscious, hug their children, sleep soundly? Would they really feel close to that perfect abstraction we call *justice* if they ignored the extraordinary circumstances of the case and locked this woman in the darkest dungeon and threw away the key? Need she remind them what those circumstances were? A quick review: depression; psychosis; hallucination; paranoia; unexpected, violent reactions . . . in brief, absolute lack of control over her actions.

Regardless of their verdict, Alice would have to live the rest of her life with knowledge of what she'd done. And with reminders of the children: their photos, their little clothes, their cribs. Their smells. You never forget the smells. And that, that constant weight would never change, no matter the jury's decision.

Alice rose to make her final statement, and abstractedly delivered the following words:

"I hope to meet my babies again somewhere, someday. I will ask them for forgiveness then. To do it here makes no sense."

A few seconds of silence follow, because the judge isn't sure whether or not Alice has finished. Now would be a good time for the defendant to burst into tears, but she doesn't cry this time, either.

That was all.

"The defendant may return to her seat."

Then the judge turns to the jury. He reminds them of their duty, advises them to take their time. Two jurors make as if to stand and the judge, perhaps in one last display of authority, testily orders them to sit back down. And so the trial ends. Not with a bang, but a gripe.

I leave the courtroom anxiously: too many people, sweaty air.

I'm not thinking about the letdown this session has been. No climax, but I don't care. My mind is on something else. Later, I'll have time to comb through the day's proceedings. But now, now I have a date.

At least I think I do. I hope I do. But I don't see him, shit, where is he, I'll wait for him at the door, but if we don't see each other, I don't have his number, oh but there he is, yes, it's him, calm down, be cool, make him come to you, that's better, pretend you didn't see him, should I get out my phone? No, that's too obvious, he's waving, I need to acknowledge him too, come on, give him a little smile, but take it easy, be cool, nothing happening here, hey, how's it going, hi, well, it's over, that's all folks, yep, just the verdict now, so you hungry? I am, let's eat then, sure, let's go, you'll have to pick the place, I don't really know this area.

5.

DELIBERATION

I remember moments of peace when for some reason
it was possible to go to the bathroom alone.

ADRIENNE RICH, *Of Woman Born*

And everything happened pretty much the way I'd imagined, because Jakes did know the area and suggested a Japanese restaurant two hundred meters from the courthouse. And when he asked if I liked Asian food, I said yes, of course, I always went out for Asian when I lived in London, pad thai one day, miso soup the next. The cheapest options in a pricey city. London, eh? What were you doing there? And thus we made our way to the restaurant through familiar terrain. As I had predicted, things were flowing and I was happy and everything was possible, until we stopped at that stupid red light and I remembered my phone, which I had left on silent all morning, it occurred to me that I should check it, a mindless impulse, a nervous tic. I knew something was wrong before I even saw the screen.

Seven missed calls: three from the daycare, four more from Niclas. And a terse message from him as well: *Call when you can.* The light turned green, but I didn't move. Nor did I look at Jakes, who was likely observing me, his new friend, with confusion. An inner voice urged me to toss the phone under a bus, but I silenced it and rang Niclas in hopes of intercepting the runaway train of my imagination.

"Don't worry, but I'm at the hospital with the baby. Something's wrong. He's got a high fever and is really out of it. I can't keep him awake."

Don't worry, says the goddamn guy. But I was worried, real worried. So worried that I said a clumsy goodbye to Jakes, sorry, sorry, I have to go, and strode with tunnel vision to where I'd parked the car. I didn't cry until I got a call from my mother, who'd heard about Erik from my father, but there wasn't much I could tell her, stiff neck, high fever, they were going to do some tests, and I didn't know more because I was far away, at a trial, no, it was even worse, I was with a man, about to eat with an interesting stranger, I had to go, I'd call her later, as soon as we knew more.

And during the sixty-five kilometers that separated me from home, I had time to think many thoughts—all ugly and dark and filled with guilt and fear.

Uluru
Dingo.
Rhodesia.
Alaska.
The Basurto Hospital San Pelayo Pediatric Ward.
What if that was the definitive title I'd been looking for?

The doctor is a professional, but also wants to establish that she's made of flesh and bone.

The doctor doesn't want you to worry too much, nor does she want to give you false hope.

The doctor wants you to understand the particularities of the case without getting too technical.

The doctor is in a hurry, she has lots of patients waiting, and she's tired, it's been a busy shift.

The doctor asks you how long the boy has been under the weather, and you want to tell her that you noticed he was feeling a little warm this morning. But you can't tell her that. How can you tell her that you suspected he might have a fever but you played dumb; that he often runs a temp but it's always just a bit of congestion, the next day he wakes up fine, much ado about nothing. How can you tell her that you packed a thermos of lentils for his lunch, brought him to daycare as usual, stripped him down to his onesie and, like always, left him in the arms of daycare staff. How can tell her that yes, you considered that he might be sick, but you told yourself *okay, if he's still warm this afternoon, I'll take him to the pediatrician, but I right now really have to run.* How can you tell her that, even with that in mind, you left your phone on silent all morning, you exercised that right. How can you explain to the woman in the white coat about Jade, Alice, the twins, the tub, the trial, the last session, Jakes, the story that was about to conclude with a big climax.

But there had been no climax in court. No, the final twist was going to transpire right here, just for me.

In this green hallway.

The saddest green hallway in the world.

Hadn't I learned my lesson? Well, I was about to receive the ultimate masterclass. Because here is the question: what does a mother have to do? Nose around courthouses, read Brazilian poetry, eat Japanese food with exotic strangers?

No. A mother has to suffer. Kneel before the cross and weep. There, her destiny is fulfilled. In that place called Golgotha. *Mater dolorosa, mater lacrimosa.*

But then, offering a reprieve, offering the basis for future excuses, the doctor says:

"It's not unusual for him to have been fine this morning.

Meningitis can develop very quickly." But she adds: "Let's wait for the test results. Try not to worry."

The jury retires to deliberate.

Erik is very thin. He always has been. I've never been able to pinch his little thighs. About to turn fourteen months old, he hardly has any hair. When we're out and about, I've rarely been told that he's a "cute kid." But people have remarked on his "adult face" or "boy's face" and then added something about his "lively eyes" to compensate. But in this hospital crib, with his flushed cheeks, with his single lock of hair plastered to his forehead, sleeping peacefully thanks to a fever-reducer, I realize again that he is perfect.

I think he is perfect.

Unfortunately, he is also my Achilles heel, an obvious weakness.

Some mothers post online that, since becoming mothers, they are stronger, more powerful, invincible lionesses, all claws, all roar. In contrast, I've never felt weaker. It's never been easier to attack me, sink me, blow me up. I have a bullseye painted on my forehead. The whole world would know where to aim. What are the internet moms talking about? No idea. Like them, I feel the same inviolable imperative to protect my child, and if I have to roar, I'll roar. If I have to use my claws, of course I'll use them. But I also know I'm powerless, more powerless than ever: my claws, my roar, are worthless against an accident, a child-snatcher in the park, a fire at daycare, leukemia, streptococcus. More doomed than ever, really; weaker than ever, with my cub at my side.

I felt pain in my deepest reaches when I saw the long needle penetrating Erik's spine. I had to turn away. Niclas held me.

The verdict was in. The spinal tap confirmed viral meningitis. In theory, it wasn't serious. We could breathe. A prize, one of the prizes I probably didn't deserve. Or a warning. The cop who reprimands you without issuing a ticket. But don't do it again, you hear? Still, they wanted to keep Erik overnight for observation, monitor his fever, which continued to be high. I called my mother, who repeated her offer to get right on a plane if necessary, but I assured her we had everything under control. I'll never know if she actually intended to come. We spent the night in diabolical armchairs placed on either side of the crib, a kind of makeshift, orthopedic Nativity. We didn't sleep. Erik did. He woke only once and I brought him to my breast, I felt his mouth burn on my nipple. Every so often, we talked about whatever we were thinking. The words sweetened the night, helped us forget our discomfort. Sometimes the baby coughed, we went quiet. He would turn over, still asleep, and we'd resume our conversation in whispers. I could still pick up on his newborn smell, the faintest trace of what it had once been. Soon, it would be no more than a memory.

"We're doing a good job," Niclas said.

"From now on, we'll do better." *I'll do better.*

In the end, Niclas fell asleep as well. His snores were sharper than usual, in that bent-neck position. He looked like a little boy. Now two were in my care. I felt very alone.

Morning came. Erik still wasn't better, he just wanted to be held, abandoned by the boundless energy that usually drove him to intrepidly explore his surroundings. We had to wait for the pediatrician. It was a different doctor than the night before, but he told us same thing: there was no course of treatment, all we could do was wait, and since the boy was still lethargic and his fever remained high, it was best to keep him for another night. It was a disappointment that immediately turned us against the doctor. We hated him. The anxiety that had dissipated now surged to mount another attack. It seemed like a twist in a Lifetime movie: at the last minute, when everything finally seems to be going okay, the blow is delivered, the mockery of fate. The aging thief who, against his will, accepts one last job before he retires and is riddled by police bullets by the end. The soldier who volunteers for a suicide mission the night before he's supposed to go on leave. The patient who dies as his discharge papers are being prepared.

I was ready to go home and be an exemplary mother. Instead, I had to go alone, shower in the midst of deathly silence, try unsuccessfully to sleep for ten minutes, return to the hospital with a clean set of clothes. When night fell, I insisted Niclas go home to sleep and I readied myself to spend a second night in the awful chair. As I sat alone in the observation room—fortunately, no other children had been admitted—my mind spun again with anguished thoughts: seizures, sudden death, a paranoid conviction that doctors weren't telling us the whole truth. That second night was the worst. Nothing gave me comfort.

But that night also passed and, after a thorough exam by the on-call pediatrician, at last we were free to go. I couldn't breathe easy until we set foot outside. On the tram on the way home, I gradually convinced myself the worst was over. We'd escaped Herod's massacre unscathed. Erik was happy again, repeating the only two words in his vocabulary:

"Mama! Mama! Bye-bye! Bye-bye!" he shouted, and half of the passengers laughed along.

My phone rang between the stops on Uribitarte and Pío Baroja. I didn't recognize the number and chose not to answer. I'd developed pretty negative feelings about that device. But the force of habit prevailed, and I picked up.

"Hey, good morning! It's Jakes. Do you remember me or what? Where are you? You missed the verdict!"

My presence in the courtroom had piqued Jakes's interest from the start. Even more so after I'd bolted on him. The truth was, he *had* thought my face looked familiar and a simple cross-reference with a girl he knew in the paper's Culture section was all it took for him to figure out who I was. Coincidentally, his colleague still had my number in her phone from an interview I'd done a couple of years ago. Jakes had asked her for it and . . . I told him he didn't have to explain and could cut to the chase.

"They accepted an exclusion from criminal liability."

"What?"

"Guilty, but she won't go to the slammer."

"That can't be possible."

"We're still waiting to hear the judge's decision on sentencing. Oh, and sorry, I haven't asked if you're okay . . . you disappeared in such a rush."

"Yeah, thanks, everything's fine, but I can't really talk right now. I'll call you later."

We got off the tram. I shrugged in response to Niclas's curious look, making light of the call. Not because I wanted to hide Jakes's existence, but because I was ready to assume my role as mother of a convalescent child, anything else was too much.

At home, Erik went down for a nap and we ordered sushi. I turned on the TV, even though Niclas hates eating in front of the screen. I had assumed the verdict from Alice's trial would be the top story, but it was the fourth or fifth news item, and rather concise. The woman who drowned her twins had been found guilty of double homicide, but relieved of criminal responsibility by reason of mental illness. Images from inside the courtroom.

Alice staring into space, hands folded. A brief statement from Carmela Basaguren, who expressed tempered satisfaction as they awaited sentencing.

Niclas seemed unaware of the news. I didn't want to discuss it, either.

I needed to think. Reevaluate my situation. I had just over two thousand euros in my checking account. About three months to finish the novel. A whole lifetime to forget what Alice had done and what the jury had declared.

Hypothesis A

When you are so controlled by your fears, you provoke them, believing that this is the way to regain the upper hand. Extreme shock therapy.

Obsessed with the twins' fragility, the only way for Alice to free herself was to do what most terrified her. Look fear in the eye and jump.

Hypothesis B

When everything has come easily, when you don't believe you deserve what you have, or simply don't value it, you can be shockingly cavalier about destroying it. This hypothesis explains both the crime and the aborted art show. By then Alice was an expert at destroying her past and starting over, as she'd proved by doing away with Jade. Basically, we're talking about the destructive power of the flipside of *the self-made (wo)man*, egocentric-capitalist slogan par excellence.

Hypothesis C

Postpartum psychosis, corollary to a whole host of undiagnosed mental disorders. Hypothesis based on time-honored scientific literature, which apparently needs no updating.

Hypothesis D

To paraphrase Uncle Ben, great power entails great responsibility. We can't discredit the wisdom of Spider-Man's uncle, but the reverse is just as true: great responsibility entails great power. That responsibility felt by anyone who holds a new life in their arms, that power. Power that, for some, is irresistible. (By the way, the original phrase doesn't come from Uncle Ben but Roosevelt, consigned to history in April 1945, shortly before his death and in preparation for the destruction of Japan.)

Hypothesis E

Conspiracy. A plot concocted by husband and wife in the interest of returning to their childless life. It's not exactly hard to imagine that two psychopaths manage to meet and marry, carry out joint plans in life and death. Once they realize that having children isn't what they'd expected, the performance begins: mother will publicly cultivate a reputation for being unstable and difficult; the almost always absent father won't improve the picture. Then society itself will decide that the acts are pardonable.

Hypothesis A requires a tragic heroine, a neglected childhood, troubled adolescence, fate sealed from birth. A part-psychological, part-mythological approach. Hypothesis B needs a sociological explanation, a review of the question of social class, maybe even a quote from Marx (material conditions determine consciousness and so forth). Hypothesis C is the objective answer of science, the unquestionable truth, the relief of jurors and the end of literature. To understand Hypothesis D, we need only mention the 1984 classic Basque film *The Death of Mikel* to conjure up the figure of the mother, all-powerful and cruel. For its part, Hypothesis E is the most fitting for the noir literary canon, and gives me the best shot at a best seller.

The truth, or what we would settle for calling *the truth*, is likely to be found in Hypotheses A, B, C, D and E, mixed together in unknown quantities.

Literature is alchemy.

Below I will reproduce a short but revealing excerpt from Jakes Ruiz de Infante's interview with Carmela Basaguren on October 27th—Sylvia Plath's birthday, and my own:

Q: You've expressed satisfaction with both the verdict and the consequences it will have in the future. What do you mean by that?

A: I truly believe this case is going to serve as an inflection point and will enliven societal debate around issues of mental illness and how it is treated with respect to criminal law. The criminal justice system's mishandling of these cases is striking, and I don't just mean in terms of material resources, but also the lack of sensitivity and foresight. It's like psychiatrists and judges are playing a game of hot potato: what do we do with the mentally ill when they commit a crime? As I've said, up until now, provisional solutions and improvisation have been the norm. This case, because of its particularities and the media attention it's received, will help change things.

Q: Following the jury's decision, the judge substituted psychiatric treatment for prison time, but opting for outpatient treatment. Alice Espanet won't even be committed to a psychiatric hospital.

A: Yes, that's correct. In my opinion, it was an excellent call on the part of the judge, who was able to detect and ameliorate the effects of a problem in our penitentiary system. There are only two penitentiary psychiatric hospitals in the whole country, and they're both very far away—in Alicante and Seville, imagine that. Alice being admitted to either one would cause serious disruption for her family. Besides, in this case, all the conditions for favorable outpatient treatment are present: Alice's stable economic situation, her husband's support . . . Moreover, various institutions will ensure that the treatment continues until Alice is fully rehabilitated.

Q: Excuse me, but . . . are you suggesting that Alice Espanet received favorable sentencing because of her social status?

A: I said absolutely nothing of the sort!

6.

ALCHEMY

I am life, and everything I touch
will be alive.

ARANTXA URRETABIZKAIA, *Why Little Darling*

Literature is alchemy. Knowledge that is prescientific, barbaric, mystical, rational, emotional, utopian, political, cold, hot, crazy, beautiful, terrible, rhythmic, chaotic, tiresome, ugly, and exhilarating. A mystery. One that—here and now—needs no answers because it asks me no questions. I write and everything finally falls into place. E-v-e-r-y-l-e-t-t-e-r.

Every breath. Every sigh. "Say goodbye to Mama!" my mother says each morning, when Erik is already buckled into his seat. And the little cub waves "bye-bye, bye-bye." He's happy to go off with the grandmother he's practically just met. My mother seems happy, too. And Niclas is definitely happy, with his surfboard, in a rush to catch waves, such a rush that he doesn't even kiss me goodbye. And most of all, I'm happy. Happy to be alone in my mother's house, I flee back indoors. It's not true, but everything is perfect: the temperature, the smell, the murmur of the ocean and this frenzied, sensual rhythm of the keys. In two or three hours, everyone will be back. Erik asleep, exhausted after playing on the volcanic rocks; my mother, fascinated, having peeked under a child's shell for the first time; Niclas, peeling nose and that wild smell, blonder than ever.

It's not true, but everything is perfect, and this perfection will end in six days. Six days and the real world returns: my mother will bid us farewell with some relief, she'll reclaim her solitude, she'll be proud of the gift she gave us and remind herself not to repeat the experience any time soon. In six days, I'll check my bank account, which will lead me to prepare for the rigors of a paying job again. Most importantly, I'll have to reread all the pages I've left behind, an awkward and unpleasant encounter. They'll be waiting for me, the living and the dead: Alice, the twins, the ghost of Sylvia Plath and her suicidal son; Australia and Rhodesia and the place called Golgotha; the wound of the woman who has just given birth, the green plastic tub. Everything I thought I could shape, though perhaps melted now, melting from the moment I took my icy eyes off them. What can you expect from this Lanzarote sun?

And in the middle of the puddle, soaked, will be the dark side of my power, my responsibility. Waiting for me, looking me in the eye, holding me accountable. The responsibility, the weight I can't shake off because at some point, more than once, I tried to put myself in her place. I've been those hands. Hands that drown kids. The mother's hands. Merciless hands. At some point, more than once, I came to understand what those hands did, or insinuated that I understood, or hinted that maybe I could come to understand (why so many twists and turns, if I wasn't led by a desire to find a way out?), and what's worse, I wanted to bring you there with me, to that miry terrain.

I came back, of course, I always come back to this side of the world, the clean realm of love and nice words, the world of mothers who pay for plane tickets and expect nothing in return, the universe of mothers who sing your son to sleep with the same song three times in a row, nights of mothers who rediscover half-dirty, half-satisfying sessions with surfer husbands, and who occasionally exchange secret-but-innocent texts with dark-haired journalists. I returned, yes, but perhaps not the same; hoping, of course, that you're not the same either, that in this dark, cramped compartment, you're as covered in muck as I am. Therein lies my responsibility, my power, my guilt.

It's a drive, a natural propensity, to narrate the mire. It has nothing to do with moral obligation or social criticism. It's something much more basic. The mire is simply there, just like Everest was there. Irresistible. Especially for those of us who are like me. Flawed. We are flawed. I am. Would life be better without the absurd impulse that pushes me to find the exact adjective for an infanticidal mother? Would everything be easier if I didn't have to devote my hours, my days, my best years to this whole practice? Would I be happier playing with what others write, enjoying the moment—suffering, forgetting, remembering the moment—not thinking about how, later, I can express it in words, in the truest possible way, for fear that otherwise it won't be real? I suspect that the answer to all of those questions is yes, but it doesn't really matter: one doesn't freely choose her impulses. To create, to destroy. Sometimes I must be a monster, bolt the door, get my hands dirty, sully more innocent souls. Not often.

At least I don't fool myself. Everything I did, I did for me. Following an impulse down to the last comma. But I want to think that, to a certain extent, I also did it for them. An acknowledgment or offering, a taste of all they were denied, a little tenderness—at least in memory—for those twins who were probably perfect too. I am life, after all. And at the end of the day, I try to beat back death.

KATIXA AGIRRE (Vitoria, 1981) has a PhD in Audio-visual Communication and lectures at Universidad del País Vasco. She previously published the short story collections *Sua falta zaigu* and *Habitat*, and is the author of numerous children's books: *Paularen seigarren atzamarra*, *Ez naiz sirena bat, eta zer?*, and *Patzikuren problemak*. She was also a columnist for *Diario de Noticias de Álava*, *Deia*, *Aizu!* and *Argia*.

KATIE WHITTEMORE is graduate of the University of NH (BA), Cambridge University (M.Phil), and Middlebury College (MA), and was a 2018 Bread Loaf Translators Conference participant. Her work has appeared or is forthcoming in *Two Lines*, *The Arkansas International*, *The Common Online*, *Gulf Coast Magazine Online*, *The Los Angeles Review*, *The Brooklyn Rail*, and *InTranslation*. Current projects include novels by Spanish authors Sara Mesa, Javier Serena, Aliocha Coll, Aroa Moreno Durán, Lara Moreno, Jon Bilbao, and Juan Gómez Bárcena.

OPEN LETTER

WWW.OPENLETTERBOOKS.ORG

OPEN LETTER

**OPEN
LETTER**